SPEEDWAY CONTENDER

BY THE AUTHOR

Burma Rifles
War Beneath the Sea
Deepwater Challenge
The Loud, Resounding Sea
Honor Bound
Speedway Contender

Speedway Contender

BY FRANK BONHAM

Thomas Y. Crowell Company

NEW YORK

Designed by Wladislaw Finne
Manufactured in the United States of America
Published in Canada
by Fitzhenry & Whiteside Limited, Toronto
Library of Congress Catalog Card No.
64-13912
5 6 7 8 9 10

TO MITCH SMITH

—who saw his first race
on a Sunday afternoon, and
has never been far
from the action since

CONTENTS

CHAPTER 1 DRIVER TEST

At one o'clock, Cotton Clark and two other students were waiting beside the Driver Education car in the high school parking lot. It was a cool January day with a clear blue sky; a few soft sea clouds drifted along the horizon. Red Hasty, one of the other students, was talking to Joanie Lane, the third.

"Just relax, Joanie—play it loose. A car is like a bicycle—point it where you want to go, and it goes there."

"But that's just it," said Joanie. "I can't even ride a bicycle!"

Cotton looked at Red and winked. "Think of something else, Red. Driving a car is like—like running a sewing machine," he said, feeling inspired.

Joanie said with a giggle: "I don't sew very well either, Cotton. I guess I'll just have to pretend I'm driving a car." She seemed not to mind at all the attention of two senior boys.

"How many hours have you had at the wheel?" Red asked her. He was a tall boy with crisp auburn hair, deep-set blue eyes, and freckled skin that was usually peeling.

"Two or three, I guess," the girl said. "My father took me out for a lesson last night, but he was so mean I quit."

"Mooney's mean, too," Cotton warned her. "But you'd better not quit. Just count on his general ignorance of cars, and keep on banging fenders till he tells you to stop. If you flunk, you can take the test again later."

The nickname, Cotton—his given name was Robert—had been apt enough when he was a towheaded youngster in grammar school, but since then his hair had darkened to a sort of tarnished blond, and he had reached six feet and filled out through the chest and shoulders. His face was square, and there was a small dent in his chin. On the bridge of his nose was a scar which, he would tell girls, was the result of an old dueling injury. The duel had been with a stone which flew up from the pavement during a drag race.

Suddenly Red muttered: "Attention, stoon'ts! Here comes Coach Mooney now!"

Cotton peered through the aisles of parked cars. He saw Mooney, who was coming along with his head down, give his stomach an affectionate after-lunch pat. Mooney thoroughly enjoyed eating. His stomach bulged out like a small kettle bolted to his abdomen; yet his arms and legs were quite thin. In Cotton's view, he was a clear case of bad design.

The coach glanced at the three driver candidates, muttered, "Hi, stoon'ts," and got straight to work. On each front door of the sedan, he hung a sign with the terse warning:

Caution: Student Driver

A similar sign was permanently fixed to the trunklid.

"Just the three of you?" he asked.

"Yes, sir!" said Cotton smartly.

His briskness attracted a suspicious glance from the instructor. After a moment the coach sighed.

"Three's enough. I might as well be driving at Indianapolis Speedway, the risks I take with you daredevils."

Joanie giggled. Cotton and Red glanced at each other. The Speedway remark made Cotton uneasy. Mooney might be working up to something about boys with fast cars being responsible for ninety per cent of the slaughter on the highways. Only a few parking spots away stood Cotton's car, a little red roadster with the sparkling beauty of a candy apple—easily one of the two or three fastest cars at La Costa High, including Red Hasty's.

Coach Mooney flipped a pencil and caught it. Then he smiled.

"I don't want anybody to panic," he said, "but you kids have to get that Driver Ed certificate to graduate, even if you've already got a driver's license like Dynamite Clark, here–" a small, ironic bow in Cotton's direction"–and I'm going to grade close. –Joanie," he said, "quit biting your lip."

"But I'm so *nervous*!" Joanie said.

Mooney winked at the boys as he said to Joanie: "Relax. I never flunked a blonde in my life."

Or a brunette, either, thought Cotton. Only boys.

The coach wrote something on his clipboard and afterward went around to check the sedan as though it were a racing car about to roar into its qualifying lap. He gave each tire a kick, then made a small *x* on the board. Cotton grinned at Red. Under *Wheels,* Mooney was probably checking: *Present.* You could put all he knew about cars into a valve cap and have room left for your lunch.

The instructor came back and regarded Cotton with his sleepy, superior smile. "How's that chargin' street machine of yours, Clark?" he asked.

Cotton tucked his hands in the hip pockets of his blue jeans. He always wore jeans and dark tee shirts because they didn't show grease.

"Little sluggish lately," he said. "I couldn't crack eighty in the school zone last week."

"Oh, that's bad! That's terrible," exclaimed Mooney. "Have you tried hand-cut slicks?"

Cotton grinned. Slicks were special racing tires. "Where'd you hear about slicks?"

"Picked it up at a race somebody dragged me to, once. Once was enough, brother! All those creeps with long sideburns and greasy fingernails–"

The other students laughed, even Red. Red had a

habit of keeping his fences mended, even if it involved fraternizing with the enemy. Cotton had to force down a bristle of irritation. But, good-naturedly, he made a show of measuring his sideburns with his fingertips, then inspected his nails. This early in the day they were still clean. He could scarcely pass a car without putting his head under the hood to see what kind of equipment the owner had hung on it. And after school there was often some boy waiting for him to put his healing touch on an ailing roadster.

The result was always more grease.

When Mooney kept grinning at him, Cotton said: "Why unload on me, Coach? Red's got a car that'll outrun mine seven days a week. He took second in the roadster race at San Luis Speedway last week."

"I'm not unloading on anybody. Only I was hearing that that machine of yours is a real highway torch. What'll she do when you open her up?"

"Smoke."

"At what speed?"

"Whatever the signs say," Cotton replied innocently. "You see, I belong to this timing club. According to our rules—"

Mooney struck his brow. "No, don't tell me! No dragging, no traffic tickets—or you can't wear your cap backwards for a full month. Right?"

"I never drag, myself. What I'm interested in now is dirt-track racing."

"You mean dirt streets, don't you?" Mooney said, digging an elbow into Red's ribs. "Like Crest Drive?"

Cotton frowned and kicked some gravel. How did

Mooney know he had received his only traffic ticket on Crest Drive, over a year ago? Thirty-five in a twenty-five-mile zone. He looked up and saw a small, malicious smile on the instructor's face.

"I've got a class at two, Coach," he said.

"I wouldn't think of making you late," said Mooney. "All right, Joanie—ladies first."

La Costa was one of a chain of small communities following the seashore from the harbor of Los Angeles to the Mexican border. The blue waters of San Diego Harbor sparkled a few miles south; Los Angeles lay a hundred miles north. Coast Highway split La Costa's modest business district with a reverberating wedge of trucks, buses, and passenger cars. Trying to turn left against that traffic, with a truck driver kicking his air brakes off and on behind you, called for the cool nerves of a commando.

Cotton waited to see whether Joanie would draw the highway or the quiet residential streets surrounding the high school. If Mooney ordered her down to the highway, Joanie would probably cover her eyes and pile into the first truck-and-trailer that came booming toward her.

The girl started the car and coasted to the exit, but when she slowed at the street she hit the brake pedal so hard that the sedan stopped dead. Mooney's clipboard crashed to the floor.

"Oh! Ex*cuse* me," Joanie said. "I—"

"Turn left," Mooney muttered.

Cotton could see Joanie relax. *Left* meant Crest Drive, on the ridge above the school, a genuine Sleepy Hollow area.

Throughout the test, Mooney was as sympathetic as a family physician. "Turn right here, Joanie," he would say. "Now make a U-turn. *That's* right. *Very* good."

When a truck loaded with workers from the commercial flower fields swung in ahead of them at low speed, the coach issued orders in a tense voice like that of a submarine skipper, until Joanie had safely passed the truck. She hooked a wheel in the dirt at the side of the road, careened back, and leveled off. Cotton and Red glanced at each other.

A moment later, apparently on a hunch that their luck might be running out, the coach said:

"Okay, Joanie. Park and turn off the engine. Red—take the wheel."

Joanie got in back with Cotton and fastened her seat belt. She slumped down, nervously depleted. Cotton nudged her with his elbow.

"You done good," he whispered. "Only one mistake: you should have taken the test next year." Joanie nodded vigorously.

The car was in motion again, heading down a long asphalt lane through avocado and citrus groves to the highway. A few blocks short of the highway, Mooney had Red turn into a side street. He kept him out of the heavy traffic until the last, criticizing his signals, warning him once about a rolling stop. Then he directed him over to the highway and Red turned north with the traffic. The highway giants thundered along, ponderous and smoky.

After a while the teacher muttered: "All right—park between those cars this side of the next light."

Red stopped, waited till there were no cars behind, then angled back and bumped the curb. He spent some time getting the wheels lined up. The right rear wheel was still welded to the curb when he cut the engine. Mooney scribbled on his clipboard.

"Clark?" he said.

"Yessir!"

"Take the wheel."

"Yessir!"

As Cotton slid under the wheel he could almost hear Mooney cracking his knuckles with eagerness. Unfortunately, the trouble between Cotton and the coach was not entirely automotive. La Costa High had recently wound up its most disastrous football season in years. It was in Mooney's mind that Cotton's ball-carrying might have made a difference.

"I'm holding a spot for you, Clark," he used to say, when Cotton was playing first string on the junior varsity. "Hurry up and put on some beef."

By last fall, Cotton finally had the beef. But by that time he had become so absorbed in building and racing cars that he had no time for football. Mooney had roared like a wounded buffalo when Cotton declined to play.

Cotton felt guilty about letting the coach down. Yet it wasn't his fault that he had a red roadster with a bored and stroked engine that devoured all his time and money. What it gave in return he could not explain, even to himself. But the thrill of building and driving such an automobile was so compelling that he was more curious than chagrined when a newly modified engine broke down. *Why* had it broken down? That was what mattered.

But Mooney hated hot rodders, and he resented talented halfbacks who refused to play football. In Cotton, he had both dislikes wrapped up in one package.

CHAPTER 2 SAY YOU'RE SORRY

Cotton cautiously let in the clutch. The car resisted him like a balky horse; he fed it more gas. With a lurch, it leaped forward. He had forgotten that rear wheel locked against the curb. He braked hard, barely averting a collision with the car parked ahead of them.

"I guess the wheel was—"

"Just drive," Mooney interrupted. "I'll turn on the radio if I want a blues song."

Cotton set his jaw and settled down to drive.

Throughout the entire test, Coach Mooney kept him on Coast Highway. Once he snapped: "Watch your speed on those left turns!"

"I was getting out of the way of that truck," Cotton told him.

"Then you shouldn't have tried to turn until it passed," Mooney said, piously.

Cotton ground his teeth and waited for the next order. This guy Mooney was a real menace. If he needled some kids this way, he'd get the whole carful of them wiped out by a ten-wheeled truck.

At last the coach said: "Turn up Arroyo Drive and head back."

Cotton swung up a narrow street mounting through green jungles of avocado groves where sprinklers whirled in the cool shade. He shifted quickly into second gear to avoid losing momentum, for the car was logy and out of tune.

"Don't speed-shift this car!" Mooney cracked. Cotton stared at him blankly. "A rodder like you ought to know what speed-shifting does to transmissions," Mooney lectured.

"Uh-huh," Cotton said.

Presently, however, Mooney seemed to soften. Settling down comfortably, he commented: "Handles well, don't she? I've got a chance to buy the car when the school gets a new one."

"Great," Cotton said. It would serve him right. The car was completely sludged up from being driven constantly at low speeds.

"For an ordinary passenger car, I mean," the coach

expanded. "When you put your foot on that accelerator—boom!"

"Yeah—just like putting your foot in a bucket of mush," Cotton said.

In the back seat, Joanie and Red laughed. Cotton knew he shouldn't have said it. But even Mooney ought to know cars better than that.

They neared a driveway where a car was waiting before backing out. Without warning, Mooney exclaimed: "*Look out*!"

Puzzled, Cotton glanced at him. They had the right of way, and the other driver was waiting; there was no problem. But if Mooney said there was a problem, then there was. He pressed the brake pedal.

Behind them, tires squealed and a horn honked.

The hairs on his neck bristled. In the rear-view mirror, he saw an ancient station wagon about to slam into them. The car was so close he could see the carbuncles of rust around the windshield. Behind the wheel was the startled face of a teen-age driver. Cotton heard Mooney's breath hiss through his teeth.

He tromped on the gas pedal, but the sedan only squatted on its rear axle to reflect on the wisdom of fast starts. "Come on, baby!" Cotton prayed, easing up on the gas to let the carburetor clear its throat. He watched the other car slide closer, rubber burning. His muscles stiffened as he waited for the clang of bumpers. Did he hear a *clink* of fenders touching? Then the pipes of his car made a hissing noise and the automobile surged forward. A gap opened between the cars. He fed the sedan some more gas and at last it took off.

Mooney slumped down as they swept on to safety. When they had a half-block lead, he suddenly sat up. "Stop this car!" he said ominously.

Cotton stopped. Mooney stared at him.

"What do they call you at the tracks?" he demanded. " 'Suicide' Clark?"

Cotton could smell burned rubber as the other car passed. He was shaking a little.

"*Never* hit the brakes without looking behind you!" Mooney said furiously.

Cotton stared at him. "But you told me to!"

"I *told* you to? I said, 'Look out!' I meant exactly that: 'Watch the traffic; hazard ahead.' "

"I *was* watching it. We had the right of way."

"A lot of dead men have had the right of way, too, but that doesn't make them any livelier."

Cotton felt suffocated by his anger. "Shall I go ahead?"

"In your state? Get acquainted with yourself. Learn your weaknesses. You aren't a good driver, and never will be. You're too emotional. I'll drive back. Practice some more and try it again."

Cotton opened the door. Then he twisted to look at the boy and girl in the back seat. "It was his fault. Isn't that right?" he demanded.

Joanie squeezed her shoulders together. "Gee, Cotton, I don't know!" she said, in a small voice. "I wasn't looking."

Cotton stared at the boy beside her. "Red? What about it?"

Red shrugged. "Don't ask me, Chief."

"Get out!" Mooney bawled.

Cotton had a wild urge to stick his fist in Mooney's face. The situation was so unjust that he could not believe it was happening. He started to get out, but then, just as Mooney began to slide under the wheel, he yanked the keys from the ignition. Mooney grabbed for them, but Cotton jumped out and hurled them across the street into a vacant lot. Stunned at his own rashness, he watched them drop into a lush tangle of milkweed. His toes curled up inside his shoes. He gulped.

Finally he recovered, pulled up his belt, and decided to finish it up in style. He turned with a grin.

"Bad pass from center, Coach," he said. "I'd better get downfield."

He trotted up the hill toward the school.

Mr. Pridmore, the vice-principal, listened while Coach Mooney explained what had happened. Cotton stood staring through a window. Mooney's deep, calm voice was the very voice of truth—except that everything he said was twisted. In the next room, a secretary was making a typewriter clatter. It was three-thirty.

"Well, Cotton?" the vice-principal said, when the coach finished. He was a fleshy man with stolid features and a long, cleft upper lip. One eye was perpetually cocked, as though a certain skepticism about teen-agers had taken up permanent lodging in his mind. But he had a reputation for fairness, and as Cotton began to talk he had a faint hope of getting through to him.

After he completed his story, the vice-principal leaned back in his chair. "There seems to be a rather large difference of opinion here," he said. "Coach Mooney thinks your stopping dead in the middle of the street could have caused a serious accident."

"Sure—and it would have been his fault!" Cotton said. "He made me stop."

"Are you calling me a liar?" snapped the coach.

Cotton shrugged and touched the toes of his shoes together.

There was a stiff silence. Finally Mr. Pridmore told Coach Mooney he might as well leave, that he would talk to him again tomorrow. After Mooney left, he said:

"Coach Mooney is hardly the type to make trouble for a boy just for the excitement, Cotton. It seems to me he must have had some reason for his action."

Cotton opened his mouth to say that Mooney did have one: that he was angry because he hadn't gone out for football. But then it occurred to him that telling the story might make him sound like a whiner who fancied he was being persecuted.

So he said, carefully, "Maybe *he* thought he had a reason. I don't know what it would be, though."

Mr. Pridmore studied him a moment. "At least we're agreed, aren't we, that students can hardly be allowed to take justice into their own hands?" he said.

"Yes, sir."

Mr. Pridmore then began voicing some cautious statements such as *otherwise good record* and *understand how your temper might have run away with you*—

"I'm not trying to make it hard on anybody," he explained, "but I won't even discuss leniency until you've apologized to Coach Mooney."

"Wouldn't that be the same as admitting *I'm* a liar?"

"Weren't you put out of a football game a couple of years ago for talking back to a referee?" Mr. Pridmore asked.

Cotton scratched his neck. "He made a bad call. The coach told me so himself."

"People will be making bad calls on you all your life. You can't go to war every time it happens. Perhaps Coach Mooney made a bad call today—I don't know. But I do know that if you won't apologize, you can consider yourself suspended."

"Suspended!"

"Certainly. I won't put one of my teachers in the position of having to take abuse from a student."

Cotton frowned at the floor, and shifted his weight.

"Well?" the vice-principal prodded.

Cotton cleared his throat. "I don't see why I—"

"In that case," Mr. Pridmore interrupted, "I'd like to see your parents here tomorrow morning."

"My father will be at the hospital. He's a doctor."

"Your mother, then. Until I've talked this over with one of them, you won't need to show up for classes."

Cotton picked up his books from the floor. Then he said, "Maybe I should ask for a court-martial."

"The way you're going," retorted Mr. Pridmore, "you're practically assured of one."

CHAPTER 3 SPIN-OUT COUNTRY

Cotton's car stood almost alone in the parking lot when he left the building. When he looked at it, all the pride they had been trying to knock out of him came up strong. The car was a "deuce"—a 'thirty-two Ford—with a Chevrolet engine enlivened by all the speed equipment he could afford. Aside from a chopped windshield, however, the car looked almost stock. It was showroom fresh, just as it had been on that day a generation ago when someone had laid down seven or eight hundred dollars and driven it down the street with its eight little cylinders of erratic horsepower proudly popping under the hood.

He started the engine and listened critically to its hoarse power song. The slightest unevenness always caught his ear. The engine growled as he rocked the accelerator; he envisioned the polished steel pistons moving under a bluish film of oil, as though the engine block were glass and he was peering into it.

He remembered how he had taken that old junker, torn it down, rebuilt it, and raced it at Ascot Speedway. But when he had finished last in the roadster event, he drove home saying to himself, *It's for sale*! He had given it all he had, and the wagon couldn't have beaten a power mower through the tall grass.

Then an old hand with cars had said, a *stock* flywheel, Cotton? Why, son, a jet engine couldn't make a stock flywheel turn over at racing speed!

So the car was all over the garage floor again, and the family complained about having to park in the driveway. But one day he turned the key, listened to the engine, and gooseflesh ran all over him. Because at last it was right. He paid five dollars to race it again, and placed third.

So here it sat now, the apple of his eye, the product of miles of lawns mowed and tons of dirty dishes washed at the local restaurants. And precisely because it was so perfect, he was in trouble.

He drove from the lot, aware of the power under his foot, tempted to blast off up the street by way of telling Mooney what he thought about him. He wished he were on a track right now. The only sure way he knew to get rid of that feeling of frustration was to take a few hot laps on a race track. But the nearest track was fifty miles away.

Then he remembered the riding club ring at Rancho Sereno, a few miles inland. He had sneaked onto the little quarter-mile track a few times when he wanted to test a newly rebuilt engine. Although the corners weren't banked, a couple of cautious laps would give you some idea of its behavior.

He turned from Crest Drive onto the county road and headed east across the chaparral-covered hills.

Fifteen minutes later, he cut onto a side road to the Rancho Sereno riding ring and polo field. The devil-grass oval was enclosed by a whitewashed fence in a grove of leafless sycamores. A creek bed passed behind the spidery gray bleachers. He stopped before the gate and glanced around. Sometimes a caretaker was down here watering the infield. But there had been rain two or three days ago and it would not need watering for a while. He dragged the flimsy gate open and drove in.

With the engine throbbing quietly, he took a couple of laps in second gear. Feeling great, he sniffed at the cold air pouring over him. The damp adobe had the rubbery feel a good dirt track should have. He kicked the car up to about fifty on the straightaways and braked for the turns, the blast of his exhausts rattling back from the grandstand. On the third lap he tried a cautious power slide, tossing the car sideways and cutting low into the corner with the wheels digging. Coming from the turn, the car skidded into the straightaway and slid for the fence. He lined his hubs up on the wall, skimming it so close that he could have reached out and pulled a board loose. The idea in cornering was to come out on a line that would take you right up to the crashwall without a lot of weaving.

His eyes watered, partly with the cold, partly with sheer pleasure. The sensation was one of maintaining control, like a seal balancing a ball on its nose—an almost impossible feat of equilibrium. Was that what it was all about, the building and the driving? For that moment of equilibrium?

His foot teased a little more power out of the engine. The car begged to be cut loose. He held it down by force of will: the formula for disaster was taking a fifty-mile turn at fifty-one. Dirt rattled against the whitewashed fence.

He was getting the rhythm, now: *run, brake, slide, run.* Come out in a slide, let your power press you back as you tore down the straightaway.

The trouble was, something was robbing him of all that power. The wheels just spun. And throwing dirt didn't win races. Was the trouble in his wheels or his tires? He had about all the bite standard wheels could deliver. What he needed was more rubber on the ground; that meant oversize wheels or bigger tires. *Wheels,* he decided.

On the next lap he stayed wide but held the throttle down a little longer. The tires took a bite as he skidded out of the turn. Elated, he powered up to the wall perfectly and held his position, feeling that he had grasped some important principle which had eluded him before.

Far back in his mind was the memory of Mooney. Mooney was nothing. He was a pot-bellied fake who needed a scapegoat for his own mistakes.

The tangy odor of gasoline fumes and hot oil perfumed the track. He pretended that he had just gotten the white flag: one lap to go! Hub and hub with another car, he was fighting it out for first place. Squeezing a little more fuel into the cylinders, he approached the back turn, holding the gas on to the last instant. The car began to slide. He swung the wheel over to correct the spin. Nothing happened.

He had crossed over that invisible line into spin-out country.

Cotton slid down as the car made a complete spin and emerged from the turn roaring head-on into the fence. He hit the brakes but the car kept moving. He ducked, as the front bumper ripped through the whitewashed boards with a splintering crash. Long sabers of wood arced through the air. Suddenly he was through the wall and skidding toward a sycamore tree.

At the last instant, the tires took hold. He slid sideways and stopped, the tree trunk crumpling his running board.

For a moment he sat behind the wheel, shaken. Then he got out and listened. All he could hear was the click of hot iron cooling under the hood. He appraised the damage to the car. A chromed headlight was out of line, its sealed-beam lens shattered. The running board was bent, and chips of whitewash speckled the fenders and hood. But the roadster had come through without serious injury. And so had he.

The fence was another matter. A dozen palings had been ripped out; the lower stringer to which they were nailed was shattered. But the wood was old and wormy, and would have had to be replaced before long anyway. He dug out three paper dollars—all the money he had—laid them on a plank and anchored them with a rock.

Then he drove quickly back to the county road.

CHAPTER 4 CAREER MECHANIC

A 'thirty-six Ford was parked in the driveway when Cotton reached home in the late dusk, so he parked in front of the house. The Ford was a lustrous black convertible belonging to Red Hasty. Blocking driveways was only one of Red's bad habits. Borrowing tools and not returning them was another. He was also a parts-scrounger who was always on the long end of the swap. Somehow, when he finally delivered his half of the trade, the pistons he was swapping turned out to be a few thousandths too small, or his kid brother had broken the crystal on the dashboard gem you had bargained for.

As Cotton walked up the driveway, Red came from the garage. Grinning, he called:

"Hey! What happened with Mr. Pridmore? I hear you got sent to his office."

"I fired him. What'd you want to borrow?"

Red tossed Cotton a spark plug. "Got any good used plugs that'll match this?"

"Not my size."

"It used to be. I thought maybe you had some good plugs left over from your old engine."

"That's right. You borrowed your last set from me, didn't you?"

"Dime apiece," offered Red.

"I'll think it over. By the way, thanks a heap for standing up for me against Mooney," Cotton said.

Red spread his hands. "Look at the spot he had me in."

"Yeah, and now look at the spot *I'm* in!"

Red started to paw through parts on Cotton's workbench. "What could I do?" he said.

"Tell the truth—that's what. There wasn't any problem, until Mooney started lying."

"Technically," Red said sternly, "it *was* your fault. You should have checked the traffic behind you."

Cotton snorted. "Technically!"

"Technically is how they book you, doc," Red chuckled, going through a drawer of parts. Cotton watched him carefully. He would not have put it past him to drop a crescent wrench in his pocket. He'd built a dragster with Red once, the first car for both of them. He had learned a lot about engines on that job, but even more about human nature. Red was always somewhere else when there was work to do.

"What'd Pridmore say?" Red asked.

"I'm on suspension. He wanted me to apologize to Mooney. I'll get a lawyer first."

"'At's telling 'em, kid. You'll wind up in Nuts and Bolts High, that way."

"Where's that?"

"Newton Boldridge High School. They teach you how to pick up trash with a stick—that's their science course. Got a good course in modern weapons, too—bicycle chains, and like that. I'll bring you hard candy once in a while," he promised.

"Bring me a dollar," Cotton said, "and you can have those plugs you're holding."

"A dollar for these bloody stumps? Keep 'em." Red dropped the plugs on the bench, probably cracking the porcelain. "I got to get home," he said, abruptly. He slid his hands flat under his belt and sauntered toward the door. "Sorry about Mooney," he added.

"If you get to feeling real bad," Cotton suggested, "tell Pridmore what really happened."

As he opened the door of his convertible, Red glanced back. "How about driving up to San Luis Speedway with me Sunday? They're having roadster races before the sprint car events. You can crew for me."

"If I go, I'll drive too, and lick the pants off you," Cotton retorted. He would like to go up, at that, although he didn't think much of the track. But there was a strong possibility that after his father heard about the trouble at school he wouldn't be going anywhere for a while. He decided to play safe.

"I guess not. I don't like the track," he said.

Red's grin split his freckled face. "What you mean is you'll be washing windows. Anyway, it's a new track; it'll pack down. You gotta learn to drive all kinds of surfaces."

"All kinds is what you get on Al Stubbings' tracks," Cotton said. "Never the same twice. Stubbings is a bum. They take more precautions against bloodshed in slaughterhouses than Stubbings takes. Herb Jacobs says a kid cracked up there last month who didn't even have a driver's license."

"Just an ugly rumor," Red said grinning. "He had a learner's permit. You've never driven there anyway, have you?"

"No, but I've watched the pileups from the pits."

"Better come on up and try your luck. See you around, delinquent."

He got in and started the car. It sounded like a go-kart. Red always had plenty of money for speed equipment, but with all his custom parts his cars never ran right, for he was a mediocre mechanic. Yet he won races, mainly because he drove like a drunken fool, and saner drivers stayed out of his way. He gunned the car, filling the street with smoke and noise, and Cotton held his nose by way of comment. The redhead laid two long stripes of burned rubber on the pavement as he took off.

After moving his car into the garage, Cotton found some rubbing compound and removed the whitish smudges left on his fenders by the fence. He forced the headlight back in line. It was past six when he finished; he smelled steak and potatoes frying in the house. A damp chill had drifted inland from the ocean. He put off going inside, because he knew his mother would take one look at him with her radar-vision and say,

"All right, Cotton—what happened?"

He wanted to avoid a Little Talk as long as possible. There had been plenty of hints lately that it was time he got interested in studies, girls, or a career—anything that did not involve an internal combustion engine.

While he was trying to decide what to do about the crumpled running board, his father drove into the garage. He was an energetic man with dark, sad eyes, but a mouth so shaped by good humor that you had to smile with him. He looked rather grim, however, as he got out and squeezed between the cars. Cotton wondered whether he had heard.

"Hi," Cotton said, grinning.

"Hi, yourself," said his father.

Cotton walked out with him and they approached the house, the doctor looking a little weary. To Cotton's surprise, he suddenly laid his hand on his shoulder.

"So what's new, Tiger?" he asked.

Cotton knew, then, that there had already been a consultation about him. He only used that little-boy appellation when he was worried about him. Mr. Pridmore must have called his mother, who in turn had probably called his father.

"Nothin' new," Cotton replied cheerfully. "Flunked my Driver Ed test. Called Mooney a liar. Got suspended. Same old stuff."

Dr. Clark laughed. "I like your sense of humor, boy," he said. "They may be making your bed at the honor farm—but you can still joke. I'll make you a deal: I won't mention it till after dinner if you don't."

"Deal!" Cotton agreed.

Dinner was being served in the family room when he returned from washing up. The room, separated from the kitchen by a counter, was large and comfortable, with a beamed ceiling and a sliding glass door onto a patio. At the far end were a games table and a dart board hanging against the wall. As his father divided the steak, Cotton's mother placed steaming serving dishes on the counter.

"Will you put these on the table, Cotton?" she asked. "My, that meat smells good! You may not need more than a cup of ketchup for a change."

She laughed. Her manner rang as false as the *ho-ho!* of a department store Santa Claus. She was an attractive woman who looked much too delicate to have produced a big-boned linebacker like her son.

"Cotton and I have a deal on, sweetie," the doctor told her. "We aren't going to talk about it till after dessert, so you might as well relax."

"Well, thank heaven!" she sighed.

After dinner, Dr. Clark refilled the coffee cups and leaned back in his chair. "Now, then," he said. "What's all the uproar?"

Cotton told him, while his father thoughtfully steepled his fingers. When Cotton stopped talking, he took a sip of coffee. "It appears that that little red speedster of yours is beginning to make trouble for you, doesn't it?"

"Why? Because Mooney doesn't like guys with fast cars?"

"Partly. I think that car is probably the source of your whole problem. But I am also thinking beyond the immediate problem. Remember that report card you brought home last semester? Could it be you were grinding valves when you should have been studying?"

"Maybe I'm one of those natural auto shop majors," Cotton said.

"Pray heaven you're not!" said his mother, with a nervous laugh.

"Oh, I don't think we need to worry about having a career mechanic in the family," Dr. Clark said comfortably. "All I'm getting at is the relationship between speed and maturity."

Cotton looked up. "*What* relationship?"

"Haven't you ever wondered why males under twenty-five pay top insurance rates? It's because, when boys are growing up, speed is what they have instead of maturity. Now, you've had this car craze for a long time, son. Seems to me it's about time you showed signs of outgrowing it."

Frowning, Cotton sipped his coffee. It was oily black and rather bitter. Something of theirs he did not quite understand, as they understood practically nothing of his. His mother reached over and gave his hand an understanding pat.

"When you're our age, dear," she said, "you're going

to look awfully odd in a red roadster with the front end lowered."

"There's a lot of top mechanics at the speedways that don't look so odd," Cotton told her. "Most of them make more money than a bank manager does, too."

"Yes, but you surely don't plan on being a mechanic all your life, do you?" his mother asked.

"Why not? What's wrong with being a mechanic?"

His parents gazed at each other in perplexity. Both started to reassure him, then stopped, and finally his father resumed.

"There's nothing wrong, of course. Personally, I respect a good, competent neighborhood garage man more than I do a hard-sell salesman. But the question is, do you want to spend your whole life in coveralls?"

Cotton thought of Herb Jacobs, who ran the wrecking yard near town. He thought of those busy, serious men, the racing mechanics, who made the grand tour of the big tracks with the top racing drivers, making in minutes major repairs on which the drivers' lives depended. They were as earnest about what they were doing as his father or any professional man he had ever met.

With a stubborn look in his eyes he said: "I don't much care what I do, just so it's with cars. I might run a shop that sells speed equipment, or head a mechanical crew at the big tracks. Or maybe design racing engines—"

"All right," his father said, with an effort toward patience. "But the *first* thing is to complete your education—and I don't mean merely killing time till they turn you loose, and getting into donnybrooks with your teachers . . . ."

Frustrated, Cotton walked to the dart board and yanked out the darts. He turned back. "Don't you believe what I told you about it?"

"Certainly, I believe it! But I think you handled the situation very badly. You did everything you could to make things hard on yourself."

Cotton threw a dart into the two-ring—far off center. "Okay! Mooney's a meatball—but *I'm* wrong because I stood up for my rights."

His father waved his hands angrily. "You don't even know what I'm talking about! Go ahead—drop out of school. Get a job in a wrecking yard. It's your life—mess it up any way you like."

Mrs. Clark laughed. "Dad doesn't mean that," she interpreted. "He just means—"

Dr. Clark stood up and carried his cup to the counter. "The devil I don't! I'm disgusted. He brings home a card full of *D*'s and low *C*'s and *now* a suspension, and talks about knowing what he wants out of life! Maybe I'm crazy. But if I can't get through to him any better than that—"

"Oh, come, come, come," Cotton's mother said, laughing. "This meeting isn't really about Life—it's about school. So stop being silly. What are you going to do about his suspension?"

His father leaned against the counter and pushed his hands through his thinning, dark hair. Cotton felt a pang of remorse, for everything that had come between them. It seemed a long time since they used to go on Cub Scout cook-outs and all. In summer, they used to sail a Sunfish together when his father could steal an hour or two from his practice. The doctor said it was the most exhilarating thing he had ever done, that it was the kind of thing that kept a man from taking life too seriously, and he felt very lucky to have a son he could do it with. But it ended when Cotton got interested in cars. Cotton felt bad about that. But—well, things changed. He sighed and threw another dart.

"I'm due at the hospital at eight tomorrow," his father said, sounding tired but controlled, now. "I'll call Mr. Pridmore before I leave home. He strikes me as a reasonable man. I'll suggest that he talk to Red Hasty and—what's her name?—Joanie. Without Mooney standing in the wings, they might tell a more helpful story."

Cotton looked at the floor. "Thanks," he muttered. Then he added: "I'm sorry, Dad. A guy like Mooney won't get off your back till he gets a fight."

"I know. There are people like that. But if you're ever given three wishes, make the first two for self-control. It'll buy you practically anything else you'll ever need."

CHAPTER 5 DIAMONDS FOR LUCK

Cotton dreamed that he was driving a screaming blue and gold racing car around the track at San Luis Speedway. It was no ordinary street machine, but a sprint car, one of those little bombs designed for one purpose—speed—without so much as a clutch to weight them down unnecessarily. He did not know how he happened to be in it. Someone, an older person, had told him he could handle it, that it was not so different from a street roadster except that it had the accelerative power of an artillery projectile; so go as fast as he wanted, but don't drive over his head . . . .

He was out ahead of the pack. For the first time in his life, he had the feeling of complete control, of razor-edged balance in the turns. Then, without warning, a front wheel dropped into a great black hole and the car was flipping into the air. He slid down under the roll bar and hit the kill-switch, and in that paralyzing instant he woke up.

His heart was pounding. It was so realistic that he would have been afraid at that moment to take a car around a track. Then the dream crumbled into ash and the cold recollection of his troubles at school closed about him.

He washed, dressed, and went into the kitchen. As he ate, his mother told him he had a date with the vice-principal at one o'clock. His father had called Mr. Pridmore, who had agreed to talk with Joanie and Red.

"I'm not too hopeful," she said. "You've put him in a difficult position."

After breakfast he did some yard chores and felt better. The sun glowed against his skin like an electric heater. It seemed strange not to be hurrying to school. He gathered up all the dead azalea blossoms in the back yard, raked the gravel path, and watered the shade plants.

At eleven o'clock, he told his mother: "I guess I'll take off. I'm going by Herb's on the way."

His mother kissed him on the cheek. "Don't worry, now. Just tell the truth. They can't punish you for that."

They can't? he thought. It all depended on whose rules you were playing by.

Herb Jacobs' wrecking yard spread over a four-acre

hilltop between La Costa and the riding club ring. Cotton drove up a long, red-earth lane through the nappy gray brush thickets. The yard was completely fenced with scrap wood, sheet metal, and old auto doors. Here and there eucalyptus trees rose gracefully from the aisles of old auto artifacts. There were whole bodies, heaps of fenders, and piles of grease-caked engine parts. It would not have surprised Cotton to drive in some day and see Herb dismantling a battleship. Under one of the trees was Herb's home—an ancient red streetcar without wheels.

He found Herb working on the front-end suspension of an old Studebaker. Lying beneath the axle, his legs asprawl, Herb looked like an accident victim.

"It's a losin' fight," Cotton told him. "A month after you get it fixed, that thing'll break again."

Herb peered out into the sunlight. "Oh—hi! Yeah, I know. But by that time I'll have it traded, see? Thought you couldn't leave the schoolgrounds during working hours."

"I got special privileges," Cotton told him. "The mob puts in the fix for me."

Herb crawled from beneath the car and wiped his hands on a piece of waste. He gave Cotton a wise smile. "They gonna put in the fix on your suspension?" he asked. He was a stocky, easygoing old bachelor with a mechanic's pallid face, and warm brown eyes. Over his thinning hair he wore a black oilcloth cap bearing the legend: *Hansen's Pistons.*

Cotton blinked. "How'd you know about my suspension?"

"Cotton, you oughtta know by now that a kid can't inflate a tire without me getting word of it." Herb tossed the greasy rag on the hood of the car. "No, the fact is your mother called me just now."

Cotton was indignant. "Why?"

Herb flexed his arms and did a deep knee bend. "To get me to put in the fix for her. Get you to apologize."

Cotton's brow furrowed. "Would *you* apologize, Herb? If somebody came up here and said, 'I don't like that silly cap you wear. Apologize!' Would you do it?"

Herb laughed. "You better believe I would—if he was from City Hall. La Costa High's a lot bigger'n you are, Rover Boy, and you're a little young for a crusade anyway. Apologize. Do it right now, for practice."

Cotton picked up a small, battered hubcap and looked at it: *Essex*. Practically a Stone Age artifact. He was tempted to tell Herb it was none of his business, but he knew he wanted to be helpful. Helpfulness was his main activity. He could always find good used parts for kids who couldn't afford new ones, and he often finished by installing them free, when a boy mechanic ran into trouble. He even built Cotton's timing club an electronic timer out of an autronic eye.

The funny thing was, he didn't show much talent when it came to building his own cars. He was always tearing down some junker he had acquired, like the Studebaker, with the idea of rebuilding and selling it. But at some point he usually ran out of gas on the project. Instead of a secondhand car, he wound up with a ton of parts.

He'd been a racing driver once, too, barnstorming

around all the big tracks. He still talked of putting a sprint car together that would open people's eyes.

"Got a set of Merc wheels, Herb?" Cotton asked suddenly.

"What's the matter with what you got?"

"They don't move the car on loose dirt."

"I'll look."

They set off on a tour of the yard. Hunting for parts here was like digging in the ruins of Troy, except that the prize was more likely to be high-lift camshafts than a gold vase. There were strange parts which must have come out of an infernal machine. They were obviously useless, but Herb kept them. One evening, just before closing time, some disconsolate customer would walk in and ask hopelessly, "You don't have a set of heavy-duty split valve locks for a 1927 Jewett, do you?" and Herb would close his eyes and try to remember.

"I don't believe I– Wait a minute! It kinda seems like–"

Then he would go prowling through the black middens of junk until he found it.

On the other hand, there were times when he could not produce even a simple item like a set of Mercury wheels.

"I don't think you really need 'em anyway," he said, shaking his head. "Too much rubber will only bog the engine down."

"Nothing could be too much at San Luis," Cotton said. "That track's slicker'n marble."

Herb snorted. "San Luis! What're you goin' up to that graveyard for?"

Cotton made steering motions with his arms and

hands. “Little driving practice. I thought I'd try it Sunday.”

“You'll get plenty of practice, Champ. San Luis is the place where an unidentified flying object is usually a wheel coming down after a crash. It could be one of yours, too, if you're going up there to work out your emotional problems.”

“Who said I was? I'm going up for some practice.”

Herb bent over to paw through some wheels. “That's good. A track is no place for a guy with a sore head. Some joker must have been trying to work off his tensions at the riding club ring last night,” he said. “The sheriff told me a car went through the fence.”

“Maybe it was a horse,” Cotton suggested.

“If it was, the critter broke one of its sealed-beam headlights. There was glass on the ground.”

Cotton smiled. “How come you don't like the San Luis track?” he asked, to change the subject.

“I don't like any track Al Stubbings is connected with. I've known the bum too long. He doesn't pay the drivers anything, and he has too many wrecks. If he could rent lions and gladiators, he'd put on a show that would throw Nero himself into a nervous tizzy.”

“It's a place to try out your car, at least,” Cotton argued, aware that he was defending the same track he'd been running down to Red Hasty last night.

“Another thing I don't like,” said Herb, “is Gil Mako in the deal. I understand he owns a piece of the track. With him encouraging kids to take chances, that track will need a resident mortician.”

“Is Mako driving again?” Cotton asked.

Mako had won the Five Hundred at Indianapolis four years before, crowning a rough-and-tumble career enlivened by big wins and spectacular crashes. A few months later, the hand he had lifted in victory as he blazed past the stands was amputated in a crash at Phoenix.

"He'll never drive in the big ones again," Herb said, "but he's gone in some sprints lately. I'd hate to try to pass him now. He'd reach right over and jab that hook of his in your eye! In the old days, I've seen him knock a boy's car right off the track if he couldn't pass him any other way."

They had reached a small shed in the heart of the jungle, the only thing in the yard which was kept under lock and key. Herb told a variety of yarns as to why he never opened it—he kept his records there; he had an enemy tied up in the shed; the family jewels were buried under the floor. He was seldom asked any more, because he seemed sensitive on the subject.

"Maybe you've got a set of wheels in the shed," Cotton suggested seriously.

Herb smiled. "Haven't you figured out why I don't demolish that old chicken coop? It's the mystery that keeps you kids coming. I might have an Offenhauser engine in there that I'm going to give to my millionth customer. Pass the word."

But when they arrived back at the Studebaker, Cotton was still without wheels.

"You're really going up there?" Herb asked.

"I think so. Probably won't qualify to race, but I'll try."

Herb sighed and dragged a tarpaulin off a small mountain of old tires. He moved carcasses until he came up with a pair of good racing tires.

"Take this set of diamonds and try them, just for luck," he said. "I'd rather see you switch tires than start fooling around with your wheels."

Cotton examined the deep, hand-cut tread. "How much?"

"No charge. All I want is a promise: let the authorities run their school without too much interference."

Cotton laughed. "Okay. But I'll give you half what I win anyway."

"At San Luis," Herb retorted, "that might leave me in debt."

"I've talked with Joanie Lane and Red Hasty," Mr. Pridmore told Cotton. "There seems to be some honest confusion as to just what happened. If you'll apologize to Coach Mooney for throwing away his keys, we'll wash out the charges and start over."

Cotton let out his breath. "Thanks a lot," he said. "What about my driving exam? Can I take it again?"

"Mr. Gulick will go out with you after school today."

CHAPTER 6 FAST HEAT

Cotton worked all day Saturday setting his car up for the races. Putting a street machine into racing trim involved negotiating a truce between the speedway and the State of California. The Highway Patrol demanded fenders, windshields, and mufflers; track rules prohibited them. Cotton had worked out a system. By removing most of the bolts which supported the fenders and running boards, he put the automobile in a state of suspended animation: a few moments with a screwdriver and he could knock off the rest of the bolts and drop fenders and running board in one piece at the track. He by-passed the muffler by removing a chromed sideplate. The headlights came off next, then the windshield brackets were detached, and the car was ready to race.

He safety-wired everything, installed Herb Jacobs' diamonds, and tuned the engine until touching the throttle was an action as sure and positive as pulling a trigger. Saturday night he took a hot bath, soaped most of the grease out of his hair and skin, and lay down on the sofa to study. His ears hummed with fatigue. In five minutes he was asleep. His mother woke him at ten o'clock and he stumbled like a sleepwalker to bed.

In the morning he pulled on his white mechanic's pants and a red tee shirt. The track fined you a dollar if you showed up in the pits in anything but white pants.

"Howsabout a lunch, Mom?" he bawled, from the bedroom.

"All right! I can hear now, you know."

When he hurried out a few minutes later, a sack of sandwiches rested on the table. "Thanks," he said. He flashed his Civics book at her. "I'll have some time to kill after I qualify, so I can get in some studying."

His mother laughed. "Oh, that's wonderful, Cotton. Will you study while you drive, too?"

"No, really—"

"All right—I don't care what you do when you're *not* driving, anyway. I'm more interested in what you do on that horrible track."

"I'll tell you the truth," Cotton said soberly. "I never drive over eighty. On the turns."

She waved wistfully from the front porch as he drove away.

Cotton drove into the dusty confusion of the speedway parking lot at eleven o'clock. The San Luis track lay in a ring of hills near the highway, fifty miles above San Diego. A fence adorned with advertisements enclosed the track. On the far side of the field a whitewashed grandstand teetered on slender underpinnings. The crashwall of the half-mile oval was backed up with earth. Behind the fence, Cotton could hear the angry explosions of engines being revved; the blatting and backfiring of cars taking practice laps at low speed; the hoarse song of a sprint car warming up. He took a deep breath and smiled with pleasure as he pulled into the double line of cars creeping through the gate onto the track.

At either side of the gate, officials were collecting fees. On a flatbed trailer at his right was a little red sprint car half buried in stacks of extra tires. The sprinters—sleek, fenderless, stripped-down, with a deep, narrow cockpit a man almost had to be lowered into—had to be hauled to the track, then pushed until the engine hit. They had one speed: fast. They were helpless until fire and nitromethane clashed with a ripping, blasting roar and they shot away. Their contours were the flow lines of the wind itself. The chromed ram tubes coming through the hood betrayed a headstrong engine's greed for fuel.

The red car went through the gate. A yellow and black roadster pulled up beside Cotton; a dark-haired youth of about twenty was behind the wheel. In profile, he had a hard chin and a somewhat flattened nose. He glanced at Cotton and winked.

"New boy?" he asked.

"Green as grass," Cotton confessed. "I drive up now and then, but this is the first time I've competed here. I had a dragster till a few months ago."

"Wear a rabbit's foot in your undershirt. This is the slickest surface south of the Ice Palace."

Cotton paid his fees, and the gate man stapled a pit pass to his belt, then thrust a canvas bag at him. He drew out a slip of paper with a 9 on it, the order in which he would drive his qualifying lap.

"Be ready when the pit steward calls your number," said the gate man. "Ever driven here before?"

"No."

"You'll have to check in with Mr. Stubbings, then." The official glanced across Cotton's car at the boy in the yellow car. "Smith—you busy?"

"I'm always busy," said the older boy, soberly but with a glint of humor in his dark brown eyes.

"Well, take five minutes of your busy day to show this boy over to Mr. Stubbings' office. He's got to sign the Articles of War."

The boy nodded. Cotton drove through the gate after him. At the edge of the track they waited while some tank trucks lumbered past sprinkling the earth. Big-wheeled pickup trucks circled the oval, packing the adobe. Cotton felt a shiver of excitement at the beautiful confusion of the infield. Multi-hued roadsters and sprint cars cluttered the bare ground called "the pits," among heaps of tires, equipment, and jeep cans of fuel. It looked like a beachhead on D Day. Men and boys in white cotton pants worked against time, every one of them convinced he could do a little better today than he had done last week.

They crossed the track and found a spot near the starting line. The boy named Smith glanced at Cotton.

"This suit you?"

"Fine."

A low earth ramp rose between their spot and the track. The other boy said the ramp was used for motorcycle jumps on Friday nights. It made a good place from which to watch the races. Cotton got out and gazed around. The old gasoline circus was in full cry. Everyone had his head stuck inside a car, was lying under it, or pouring fuel into it. Cars were warming up with a hard staccato thunder. An Offenhauser split the air with a deafening screech.

Home again! Cotton thought blissfully.

The other boy came over. He was a full four inches shorter than Cotton, but looked cool and confident. "Bud Smith," he said, offering his hand.

"Cotton Clark."

Bud rocked his thumb toward the area at the far end of the stands. A large house trailer rested in the shade of a shabby pepper tree. "The trailer is headquarters," he said. They went through a gate before the bleachers and approached the trailer. "Where you from, Cotton?" Bud asked.

"La Costa."

"I'm from San Diego County myself. I go to City College—half days, that is. I work in a body shop, afternoons."

Reaching the house trailer, Bud rapped on the screen door.

"It ain't locked," a man called.

They entered a cedar-paneled room with a blue carpet and expensive furniture. Everything was surprisingly luxurious for a speedway, where living was traditionally primitive. A very pretty girl wearing pale blue shorts and a white sweater smiled at them from a sofa. Beside her sat a stout man in a white shirt and pants. At a desk, a lean, red-faced man with ice-blue eyes and curly blond hair was staring at them. Cotton recognized him: Al Stubbings. He had been seeing Stubbings around race tracks for years. Stubbings was said to own an oil well somewhere, and kept three or four racing cars in action around the country. It was generally understood that in a business deal he could draw blood as neatly and greedily as a six-foot mosquito.

"What's the problem?" Stubbings asked.

"No problem," said Bud Smith. "This is Cotton Clark. He hasn't competed here before. The gate man said he was supposed to get The Word."

Stubbings drew a printed form from a drawer, pushed it toward Cotton, and dropped a pencil on it. "Just a release," he said. He gave Cotton a brief, mechanical smile.

Cotton signed it. Stubbings scrutinized his signature,

put the paper in the drawer, and sat back. He waved a hand at the couple on the sofa.

"Meet our trophy girl—Sandy Stevens. Sandy's in the flicks. And my pit steward—Mel Franks."

The girl gave Cotton a gleaming smile, but Franks seemed to have difficulty trying to appear pleasant. He had a ripe, pudgy face and neat gray hair.

"When I call your number for a race, you jokers better be ready," he warned. "Don't be changing tires or setting the spark up. This is one track where things run on time."

Cotton and Bud nodded gravely. All pit stewards lived in a state of panic, as though they had one more event to run off before the world ended.

"What's the purse today?" Bud asked Stubbings.

The lanky promoter crossed one leg over the other. "There's two heats for street roadsters, and I'm losing money on both," he said. "That's right from my bookkeeper, kids. He tells me I'm a sentimental fool not to discontinue them. But I figure a boy's got to start somewhere, and I'm going to run them as long as I can. The prize is twenty-five bucks for the fast heat, a case of oil for the other."

Bud groaned. "I burn up a case of oil every time I race, Al!"

Stubbings sighed, his red face unhappy. "I wish I could do better. What I *can* promise is that if you kids keep putting on a good show every Sunday, the attendance will soon justify purses I won't have to apologize for. You may be paying income taxes by next fall."

They laughed. The fact was, Cotton knew, that Stubbings was making money on the roadster races or he'd have discontinued them before now.

"If it makes you feel any better," Stubbings went on, "the purse will be fifty per cent of the gate two weeks from today. It's our anniversary. Depending on the crowd, first place in the fast heat should be worth about three-fifty."

Mel Franks assigned them numbers, and they left.

CHAPTER 7 OLD PRO

When they returned to the pits, a trim little gold and blue sprinter had been parked next to their roadsters. Three mechanics wearing white trousers and peppermint-striped shirts were working on it. There was no joking or horseplay among them: they were as serious as businessmen, which, in a sense, they were, for they were professional racing mechanics. If their driver burned up an engine, they would have it rebuilt by the next morning. If the track surface were too heavy, they would change the rear-end gear ratio in minutes.

Bud pointed out the name beside the cockpit.

Gil Mako

"Keep your ears open," he said. "Maybe we'll learn something."

"Mako's quite a boy," Cotton agreed, without enthusiasm. Perhaps Herb had conditioned him against Mako and his rough-and-tumble style; he was more inclined to think of him as a lucky freak than as one of the greats.

"I don't mean Mako," Bud said. "I mean his mechanics. They're the best in the business. Personally, I wouldn't give Mako track space. He's a menace."

A black roadster came wheeling in through the dust, exhausts roaring. It was Red Hasty's Ford. Beside Red sat a burly, black-haired man with a weathered coppery face. As soon as the pair got out, Cotton recognized Gil Mako. The Old Pro was wearing a blue jacket with red seams and black Wellington boots. He called to one of his mechanics.

"Jimmie, set up the timing on this car a whisker, will you?" Then he slapped Red on the back. "You just wheel her like you did last week, kiddo, and you'll be in the trophy dash before you know it. I like your style."

Hasty filled his chest. He was so high on Mako's praise that he would probably go right out and flip over the crashwall. As Mako turned to walk toward his crew, Red saw Cotton. He said quickly:

"Gil—would you look over this boy's wagon? He's a buddy of mine—Cotton Clark."

Mako glanced at Cotton. He gave him a deadpan stare; then, hands in his pockets, he walked around the car looking as judgmental as a used-car appraiser. Cotton was at once pleased to have the opinion of an expert, and resentful at Red for using him to show off: *Me and the Old Pro are just like that* . . . . That was what the gesture meant.

Cotton said quickly: "If you're too busy, Gil—"

Mako did not reply. His dark and jaded eyes, set into the lined leather of his face, seemed to pick at the car as he walked about it. Nothing in his driving record belied the look of rashness about him. He was probably the last of the old-style chargers, who had blasted through the pack with cold-blooded disregard for their lives or those of anyone else. But they could all drive like demons, and at one time or another Mako had taken all of them. He had been winning races against the new breed too—the cool, steady, less flamboyant drivers—when the loss of his hand put an end to big-time competition for him.

Mako finished his inspection of the car's exterior, stuck his head in the cockpit, then turned to Cotton with an expression of surprise. "Don't you know what this heater needs, son?"

Cotton was impressed and eager, despite himself. "No, sir."

"Satin lining, and lilies on the hood. Where's your shoulder harness?"

Red laughed. Cotton's eagerness wilted. "I haven't hooked it up yet."

Mako smiled crookedly. "Otherwise I guess you're okay. What was that name?"

"Cotton Clark."

Mako said in his rough way, "Hiya, Cotton," and extended his hand. No—not his hand: his hook. Two steel prongs extended from the sleeve of his jacket. Cotton grinned and accepted the handshake. A vise closed on his fingers. He yelped.

"Ouch!"

Red slapped his leg. The mechanics chuckled, while Mako smiled steadily into Cotton's eyes, until Cotton panted,

"Hey—that hurts!"

Mako released him, pretending to scowl at his mechanical hand. "This fool contraption—! Can't seem to get used to it. Sorry, Cotton."

"I'd say you were doing all right," Cotton said wryly.

Mako looked at Bud Smith, who had observed Mako's antics without smiling. "How's the king of the consolation races?" he asked Bud, with a grin.

"You're not kiddin', either." The little dark-haired driver sighed. "If I go in the consy once more, I should win a perpetual trophy—say a silver tow rope."

Mako strolled over to Bud's roadster and kicked a front tire. "Where'd you get this freak front end?"

"A shop in San Diego makes them. R. C. Cunningham is the manufacturer."

Mako squatted to dig some grease from the drag-link with a pencil point. "Never heard of him. Maybe that's your trouble, kid. These spring perches are right out of Junk Yard Alley."

Bud jingled some coins in his pocket. Obviously he was annoyed. "A lot of guys are using them, Gil. No wrecks yet."

"A lot of guys are driving cars with cracked axles, too.

Who's Cunningham? Some Little League engineer with a lathe in his basement?"

"He's a high school shop teacher. This is a sideline."

Mako stood up. "I believe it. Better get something standard, or they'll be scraping you off the track one of these days."

". . . All the wind isn't in Texas," Bud told Cotton disdainfully, after the big driver had left. "You can't *buy* a better front end than that. I used to have an auto shop class with Mr. Cunningham in high school. He works to closer tolerances than most of the big shops do. He gets about sixty dollars for these, and I don't think he makes a nickel on them. All he gets is the satisfaction of knowing some boy isn't going to get killed because he couldn't afford two hundred bucks for a good front end."

Mel Franks, the pit steward, came loping by with a watch in one hand and a list of drivers in the other.

"Fifteen minutes!" he bawled. "Warm up and get in line for your qualifying laps."

Each driver would take a single lap at his best speed. The fastest cars would compete in the fast event; the rest went in the slow heat.

Bud took a bottle of white shoe polish from the trunk of his roadster and painted a big *11* on the door of his car. Cotton borrowed the polish and drew a *14* on his roadster, the competition number he had been assigned by Mel Franks. He listened to Bud's engine warming up. It sounded lazy and uneven. He was surprised, because it was loaded with custom equipment. He started his engine, then stood back pulling on his flameproofed coveralls and helmet while he listened to it. Half his mind was already out there on the track. He yawned; he was always sleepy just before a race.

"Nervous?" Bud asked, as he pulled on a red and black helmet.

"Who, me?" Cotton retorted indignantly; then grinned. "Darned right I am. Too scared to drive; too proud to back out."

"You'll loosen up after the first lap. Then you won't want to quit. Have you raced before?"

"Sure. And the more I race the less I like it. Explain that to me."

"I can't explain it," Bud said, "but I can give you some advice: don't race if you don't like to. It's the guy that's afraid who gets hurt."

Cotton nodded agreement. "Well, I don't mean I'll panic. But some drivers are naturals, some have to learn. For me, the fun is building the cars. The only reason I race is to see what the car will do."

"You can find that out on a drag strip," Bud told him.

"Not the things I want to find out. I'm interested in the whole package. You can't run a road test except in a turn with the throttle honked on."

"Takes all kinds, I guess. Myself, I only build 'em so I'll have something to drive."

The loudspeaker crackled. They fastened their safety equipment and wheeled over to the track to get in line.

Cotton kept thinking about Bud's remark: "It's the guy that's afraid who gets hurt." There was a lot of truth in it. The anxious driver tended to make more mistakes; he touched the brake when he should have kept feeding the gas, and spun into the wall. But Cotton was catching on, and meantime he took no unnecessary chances and was learning the things you could only learn behind the wheel.

The roadster at the front of the line dug out; something in the ragged note of its exhausts made him look up. It was Red, looking tense and dwarfed in his gold helmet as he streaked down the straightaway for his warmup lap. He made the oval fast and shot under the green flag.

Cotton frowned as he watched Red slide into the turn. He was hitting it much faster than usual—the Mako influence, probably. With his big tires biting, he blasted through the turn. Cakes of adobe flew from his treads. He came out with a ripping, blasting roar and blazed down the back straightaway. He skimmed the crashwall without an inch to spare, set the car up fast and skidded into the final turn. Cotton twisted quickly to watch him come out of it. He was driving like a fool. That stuff was all right for the veterans; but he was no veteran. He came out in a whining slide, jittered around for a moment on the feather-edge of disaster, and went under the checkered flag.

The track timer announced that Merle Hasty, in the Number Six car, had turned in a time of twenty-four seconds. It was good, but it had looked and sounded better than that. The really skilled drivers did it so quietly and smoothly that you scarcely realized it when the records were set.

Now Cotton was at the head of the line. The starter motioned him out onto the track.

He drove his warmup lap at fair speed, getting the feel of the track. It was too dry, inclined to be slippery. He was still trying to decide how hard to shove the throttle when the green flag flashed in front of him and he bit his lip and kicked the gas pedal all the way down.

The roadster nearly jumped out from under him. Those tires of Herb's gripped like suction cups. He could feel the car trying to fishtail on the rough earth. The turn rushed at him as though it were on rails. He cut power, twisted the wheel, and tossed the car into a slide. As the front end pointed across the horseshoe, he floored the gas pedal again and went through the turn jerkily, making a dozen little corrections. He was pleased with the way the car responded; yet he realized he was driving like a beginner. Coming out, he opened up and did a long slide up to the wall. For an instant he thought he was gone: he was going to collide and go into a ruinous spin! But the extra gas he poured on straightened the car out just a few inches from the planks.

He took the back turn higher and slower, flattened his throttle with his wind-scalded eyes streaming, and came out perfectly. His pipes cannonading, he went under the checkered flag and coasted into the infield. He reached up to wipe his eyes, and discovered he had forgotten to pull up his goggles!

He grimaced. That was what Bud meant about not driving if you were afraid to. He had been so nervous he had forgotten to adjust his goggles.

He heard his time announced as Bud went out.

Twenty-five and a half seconds. Not bad; certainly not good. He would do well to make the fast heat.

From the infield, he watched Bud take an easy warmup lap. So easy that Mako, having a cigarette with Mel Franks, commented sourly:

"Stand by with the coffee, Mel. He's fallen asleep."

"Real smooth chauffeur, though," the official said.

"So is molasses smooth, but it don't win races."

But even Mako straightened a little when the yellow roadster slid from the back turn in a long whining power skid. There wasn't much snap in that engine, but it was delivering all it had when Bud went across the starting line. As he headed into the front turn, Cotton kept waiting for him to cut the power. He seemed to keep charging forever. Cotton winced and waited for the slide, the thud, the loud, clanking crash. At the last second, Bud set the car up gracefully and powered into the turn. He went high and stayed inches under the wall. The roadster revealed its basic sluggishness when he came out of the turn and gunned into the stretch; it dragged up to its maximum speed with frustrating slowness. Again Bud held the power on until the last second, making time where he could. He took the back turn almost at full power, came out sideways and hurtled toward the wall. Smoothly he came around and ran under the checkered flag.

The announced time was twenty-six plus.

"That ain't bad, considering what he's ridin'," Mel said.

Mako snapped his cigarette onto the track. "You

kiddin'? There isn't enough spark in him to light a trash fire. I like a kid that goes out there and gets himself a ride. Smith drives like he was waitin' for the lights to change."

Eat your liver, Mako! Cotton thought happily. In a sprint car, Bud could give you all the competition you want, and you know it.

For all his being head-high to a roll bar, Bud Smith had the kind of timing and judgment seldom seen except at big tracks.

When lap times were posted, Cotton had made the fast heat by a split second. Red Hasty's time was second best. And just to prove that talent wasn't everything, Bud was down in the dusty clash and jangle of the consolation cars once again.

CHAPTER 8 GRUDGE RACE

The speakers called for the slow heat contestants. Two abreast, the cars cruised the track, their exhausts spitting raw fuel with loud explosions. They bunched close together, waiting for the green flag. With their leather masks pulled up—protection against flying gravel and clods—the drivers looked slit-eyed and sinister. After two laps the starter turned them loose.

The first ten seconds of the race were the usual slapstick comedy, with overtones of tragedy. Nero would have wanted it this way, Cotton thought.

In a wild eruption of noise, the two lead cars raced

into the turn, locked wheels, and hit the wall. The yellow warning lights went on; the yellow flags fluttered.

When the wreckage had been dragged off the track the race resumed, with Bud holding fourth place. A veteran of the consolation races and the frantic slow heats, he drove cautiously, pressuring the car ahead. He waited until the car took a turn too high, then scooted under him.

Now he was crowding the number two car. He stayed on it until the driver, getting nervous, took a turn too fast and spun out. Bud rammed into the hole, stayed on the rail, and skidded out of the turn in second position behind a blue roadster. Cotton yelled encouragement as he roared by.

But the driver in the number one car stayed low and shut Bud off. Only a faster car could pass by going wide, and Bud's problem was lack of power. As they got the white flag for the last lap, Cotton wondered what a driver like Bud did when he couldn't pass without taking a risk. Settle for second place? But that wasn't what racing was all about: a real speed chauffeur drove to win.

As they charged into the last turn, Bud began "nerfing" the other car—jolting it with his front wheels enough to let the driver know he still wanted to pass. The other man responded with a snarling burst of power—and started to spin out. Bud had teased him into taking a chance. Daylight opened between car and the rail, and Bud shot into the gap. Coming out with a good lead, he cut the blue car off and slid for the fence.

He still had a half-length lead when they roared across the finish line.

Cotton pounded him on the back. "The best chauffeur and the worst car in the race! What a combination!"

"Thanks a heap," Bud said, grinning as he pulled off his helmet and mask.

"Why don't you work that wagon over?" Cotton asked earnestly. "It's set up too tight. Can't you hear it? And your carburetors wheeze as if you're running on kerosene."

Mako and Hasty came over. The redhead was already dressed for his race. Mako watched Bud wipe the sweat from his face. "What do your friends call you—'Lucky'?" he said.

"What's lucky?" Bud retorted. "I wrote the play, and he said his lines just right."

"Nine drivers out of ten would have had the brains to keep the hole plugged on you," Mako scoffed.

Bud glanced at him with a frown of irritation. For a moment Cotton was puzzled by Mako's sarcasm; it seemed like the behavior of a man eaten up by jealousy. But of what was he jealous? Of a beginner's ability to look like a champion even in a third-rate machine?

Suddenly Cotton realized that was the whole trouble: Mako was over the hill; Bud Smith was on the way up—and making a reputation for himself by driving the kind of race Mako had always scorned.

When Bud winked, Cotton knew that he, too, understood the situation. That was why he could take Mako's ribbing good-naturedly. Cotton watched Bud roll his shoulders to work out the stiffness as he told Mako:

"I knew how that guy would drive a race when I watched him take his qualifying laps. He likes to drive a high turn, so I made him take them low. Then I encouraged him a little and he spun out."

"Well, isn't that fascinating?" Mako said, nudging Red.

Red pulled his goggles over his head and left them dangling around his neck. "How do you figure me, genius?" he asked Bud.

"Oh, I couldn't tell you that," Bud said seriously. "I might drive against you sometime."

Mako uttered a laugh. "On your best day you'll never drive against Red."

"Not in that car," Cotton agreed, looking at the yellow roadster.

"Not in *any* car," snapped Mako. "Red's a real goin' driver."

"Don't encourage him," Bud said. "He's crazy enough as it is. —Excuse my language, Red."

Mako jabbed his steel hook into Bud's chest. "Let's get something straight, Shorty. Crazy, and gutty, are two different things. Suppose that boy hadn't let you bother him? How would you have got past?"

"Stayed on his tail and kept him sweating. Sooner or later, he'd have squirreled out."

"Not later—*sooner*, because you only had one lap to do it in. So what if he didn't squirrel out? That's what I'm askin'."

Bud frowned, thinking about it; and maybe, thought Cotton, not wanting to give away future strategy.

"If he was you, Gil," Cotton said, "he'd have climbed right over him. It wouldn't be the first time. Guy told me they invented standoff bars to protect the racing public against Mako."

Mako actually looked pleased and flattered. "And that's the truth, kid! I'd work in close and go right over his wheel. Dump him on his tailpipes. There he was trying to figure out what hit him—and there I was up front!"

Red kept looking at Bud. "How about it? What if he hadn't let you pass?"

"There's always tomorrow," Bud said, with a smile.

"Tomorrow? I never heard of it," Mako snorted. "With me, it was always today. I never heard of them running the Indianapolis Five Hundred any day but Memorial Day."

Mel Franks came hurrying past, his face red and his armpits ringed with perspiration. "Warm up that wagon and get in line, Clark! The fast heat's coming up."

As Cotton reached for his helmet, Red held his arm. "Wait a minute, Cotton. You claim there's nothing wrong with Bud but the car he drives, right?"

Cotton saw it coming: a grudge race. He glanced uneasily at Bud; it seemed as if a light had been turned on inside Bud's head which gleamed out through his eyes. Bud knew what Red was going to suggest, too, and he was eager for it.

"In a good car," Cotton said, "nobody around here could take him."

Red grinned broadly. "Okay. Let Bud drive your car in the fast heat. Bet a valve cap I take him."

Cotton looked at Bud. "How about it?"

Bud shook his head. "No, thanks. I don't like driving other guys' cars. Suppose I pile it up?"

"You won't pile it up. At least there'd be less chance of a crash than if I were driving."

Bud rumpled his black hair, seeming tempted almost beyond his strength.

"Go ahead," Cotton urged him. "Take a couple of extra laps before you let them bunch up. Get the feel of it."

"Is it legal?" Bud asked Mako.

Mako gestured with the hand that held his cigarette. "Why not? It's the car that qualifies, not the driver. But I'm warning you—you'll be sorry."

Bud pulled on his helmet. "If I'm not back by five o'clock, don't wait dinner. I may decide to win the trophy dash too."

At San Luis, the inverted-start system was used: the slowest cars started in front. Since Cotton had qualified with the poorest time, his car started "on the bubble"—in the front row and on the rail. Cotton found a place on the motorcycle jump from which he could see both turns and the starting line. Excited and nervous, he watched the eight cars backfiring about the oval in close formation. Every now and then Bud would make a little sprint to try out the car's acceleration. The other drivers had to catch up.

Now the cars were bunched close, with Bud setting a fast pace to offset his disadvantage in acceleration. The pack charged from the back turn; the green silk came down in a rippling slash.

The roar of eight engines opening up reverberated through the stands as the cars thundered into the turn. Hub to hub with another car, Bud headed through. Each pair of cars made precisely the same moves; the distance between their spinning wheels was inches—at eighty-odd miles an hour!

By the end of the third lap, positions were being traded. With two cars forcing him hard, Bud stood them off to hold his lead. Red bullied his way up to third place. His philosophy seemed to be that if you appeared willing to crash rather than give way, other drivers would make room for you. He was using that strategy now on a driver named Jimmie Martinez, in second place. Martinez held steady under Red's dangerous tactics for several laps, but finally, unnerved, began to speed up. Cotton could tell that he was driving over his head.

On the eighth lap, as Bud went into his slide for the turn, Martinez tried to squeeze between him and the rail. Cotton tensed, as the cars touched. Bud was thrown into a wild spin toward the crashwall. Spectators on the raised bank scattered and a yell boomed from the stands. Fighting the wheel, Bud succeeded in controlling the spin, but slid along with the tail of the car almost scraping the fence.

Martinez slowed momentarily to avoid colliding with Bud. In a flash, Red gunned past him. He obviously thought he was going all the way to the front, but Bud recovered and nailed the throttle down just in time to sprint ahead.

Red was back in the clods again, with two laps to go.

Suffocating with excitement, Cotton took a breath and tried to settle down.

Bud kept driving his same hard, smooth race. While Red toured the straightaways with a scorching shriek of power, sawing away at the wheel in the turns, the black-haired boy set his car up precisely and anchored the wheel. A baby could have slept beside him. Somewhere near Cotton, Mako was bawling advice. No wonder he didn't like Bud's style! Bud made a difficult trick look too easy.

The white flag: Red crowded it on and risked a crash to pass outside. Bud cut him off. Red swung inside and began wildly jarring at the rear of the roadster.

Cotton muttered. The idiot! Without standoff bars, Red could do nothing but cause a smashup. Bud glanced back and gave an impatient shake of his fist as Red forced him into the last turn at impossible speed.

Then, a few lengths short of the turn, he swerved and hooked a front wheel in the loose dirt at the edge of the track. Dust flew into the air, dense and blinding. Unable to see, Red veered wide, completely engulfed in dust, and momentarily disappeared. Bud blasted on through the turn as Red emerged from the miniature dust storm in a flat slide at low power. He braked, fishtailed, and opened up again with a roar of his pipes.

But he was too late. The red car crossed the wire a full three seconds ahead of him.

CHAPTER 9 PARTNERS

Spattered with mud, the two cars pulled into the pits. Bud had peeled away several sets of protective cover-lenses from his goggles to keep his vision clear. Cotton pounded him on the back as he pulled off his mask and helmet. Bud was laughing. Nearby, Gil Mako watched somberly as Red set the brake and piled from his car, white with anger. Red started to speak to Mako, then yanked off his helmet, ripped away his mask and strode up to Bud.

"What a stinking way to win a race!" he choked.

Bud lowered the bandana with which he was wiping

his face. "You don't like dust?" he asked, surprised.

Red flung his helmet on the ground. "I couldn't even see where I was at!"

"Well, as long as you stay in the dust," Bud counseled, "you know you're still on the track."

Mako couldn't stay out of it. He walked over. "There's a rule against that trick, buster. I'll bring it up at the Association meeting this week. You'll be lucky if you get your check."

"It was Red's party," Cotton retorted. "It's his own fault if he didn't like the games they played."

Red looked as though he were about to swing. Tears of anger brimmed in his eyes and his freckles stood out on his face. He stood inches taller than Bud, and might feel that he had the edge in manpower. But Cotton noticed that Bud was set for him. Maybe that was what cooled the redhead down so fast. After a moment he picked up his helmet and slung it into his car.

"Ever try that again, I'll run the wheels off you," he muttered.

"All right, forget it," Mako said. "I'll take it up with the track steward Wednesday night.—Come here a minute."

Red walked over to Mako's blue and gold sprinter. The mechanics had paid no attention to what they obviously considered a kids' argument. They were too busy readying a car for a race.

"Climb in for a minute," Mako ordered. "I want to see something."

Charlie Grimes, Mako's head mechanic, glanced up with a frown. He was a gray-haired man of about fifty who wore round gold-rimmed glasses and looked like an accountant, except for his hands. Cotton had the thought: Mako's going to let him drive it! But of course that was impossible. Turn a green driver loose in an Offie-powered speedster in the trophy dash? Even Mako had better judgment than that.

"What's the idea?" Grimes demanded.

"Just set tight, Charlie," Mako told him. "Go on, Red—climb in."

Red squeezed into the cramped cockpit, almost disappearing when he sat down. Red was no midget, but the car had been cut to Mako's oversize dimensions. The boy's red hair barely showed above the cowling.

"How's it feel?" asked Mako.

Red chuckled nervously and stretched himself up. "I feel like a pygmy in a bathtub. Don't pull the plug—I might go down the drain."

"Can you manage the pedals?"

Red squirmed around. "Well . . . ."

"We'd have to block everything up a little," the veteran said thoughtfully. "Know that purple and white sprinter of mine?"

Red nodded. "The Braggan Special?"

"Right. Why don't you come up next Saturday and tool it around while the track's not being used?"

Red sat back. "You're kidding!"

Charlie Grimes muttered, "We've got to warm this car up, Gil."

"Okay—hit the silk, Red. Just thought you might like to see whether the sprints are your dish. If you can handle it, I might let you drive it a week from Sunday."

Red was incoherent. The Braggan Special was no tired old rail job: Mako had gone an entire season with it on the Eastern circuit a few years ago. It might be basic in some areas, but it would do fine until rocket-powered cars were invented.

Red blurted: "Gosh, Gil, I—!"

Mako patted his shoulder as he climbed out. "If you can handle it," he said casually, "we'll work out something on splitting the purses you win, in case you'd like to drive it regular."

Red rubbed his neck. He lowered his voice. "You have to be twenty-one, don't you, Gil?"

Gil playfully stuck his thumb in Red's ribs. "You're twenty-one, Red. I've got a paper in Al's office that proves it. All you have to do is sign it."

Bud turned away and walked to his car, his face somber. Cotton watched him commence stowing tools and equipment in the trunk of his car. He looked around.

"Get the picture?" he said.

Cotton nodded. "Sure. The Old Pro wants you to feel bad. He doesn't like having his protégé finish back in the clods. So he puts Red in a sprint car."

"Where'd you ever meet this character?"

"I grew up with him. Cub Scouts, Pony League—the whole bit. We even built a dragster together a couple of years ago. Red's all right. He's got a low boiling point and a big mouth, but—"

Bud smiled. "But otherwise he's a doll."

Cotton scratched his head and tried to figure it out, about friends. "I guess that's about it. Friends get to be a kind of habit. Maybe that's the way I am about Red. Sometimes I could shove a piston down his throat. Other times— Say, how'd you like the way my car handled?" he asked.

"Fine. Best ride I ever had."

"You're kidding," Cotton said.

"No, I mean it. It handles just right."

"Like to drive it every week?"

Bud set a tool box in the trunk. "Now, don't do anything rash just because you're mad at Mako."

Cotton shook his head. "All I want is to win races. With me at the wheel, the car hasn't a prayer. And with you doing your own mechanical work, you're lucky to finish under your own power."

Bud walked over and looked into Cotton's roadster, then glanced around. "You serious?"

"Why not? Driving and car building are two different talents. You've got a good engine, but it's set up too tight. I've got a car that handles right. We could rebuild your engine and put it in my car. Maybe that would be the winning combination."

"I couldn't help much with the work," Bud said. "I'm going to City College, you know, and working part time."

"If I needed a mechanic," Cotton said, "I'd be talking to Charlie Grimes. You can help week ends, if you want."

Cotton felt warm and gooseflesh. In his mind, he was already tearing down Bud's engine, getting ready to graft it onto his chassis. Then the dream widened to include the sprint car they would some day build.

Bud offered his hand. "Let's try it."

Cotton shook his hand. "When can you start?"

"How about tomorrow night? I'll bring my machine over. We'll have to trade cars."

Cotton nodded. "You ought to drive the competition car and get to know it."

Driving home that night, he had the feeling that all his life had been a mere warmup for what was ahead. He had a faith as strong as a missionary's in his and Bud's ability. What if they were only talking about building a roadster?

It would be a sprinter next year, or the year after . . . .

Somewhere, the owner of a racing car was getting tired of arguing with his wife; he had promised to give up racing after they were married, and now here they were with two children and he was still driving.

"It's us or the car," she was saying.

It happened all the time. All you had to do was to save your money and keep your ears open . . . .

CHAPTER 10 DRAG STRIP FINAL

When Cotton's father arrived home Monday night, he stopped in the driveway and stared at the two roadsters crammed half in and half out of the garage. Black with grease, Cotton crawled from under one of the cars. He had not explained to his parents about Smith & Clark. Such news always provoked a question-and-answer period about how soon the family car could be parked in the garage again.

Dr. Clark gazed into the garage, and passed his palm across his brow. The cars looked as though land mines had exploded under them. The hoods and fenders were off. Parts were soaking in black buckets of solvent. A radiator lay on the floor. Bud came from the workbench.

"Uh, Dad, this is, uh, Bud Smith," Cotton said uneasily.

Bud wiped his palm on his pants, then dropped his hand. "Pleased to meet you, Dr. Clark. I'll shake hands with you next time."

"That's all right," Dr. Clark said amiably. "What are you boys up to?"

Cotton explained what they were up to.

"About when will I be able to get into the garage again?"

"We're trying to get through by a week from Sunday."

"Well, I certainly wish you luck."

"I'll dust your car off every day," Cotton promised.

Dr. Clark made a wave of resignation and trudged into the house. In a few minutes, Cotton's mother came out.

"Will you stay for dinner, Bud?"

"No, thanks. I'll go up town and get a hamburger. I'm too dirty to come in."

"We have special chairs for grease monkeys," said Mrs. Clark. "It's time to wash up, though."

After dinner, Cotton's father called him into his study. "Wasn't there some nonsense about finals this week?" he asked.

"Yes, sir."

"Well?"

"So I'll study. I studied a little this noon—"

"Is that how you plan to prepare for your finals? Twenty minutes a day over a sandwich?"

"No. But—we've got to keep going on this so we can put the cars back together in time."

"In time for what?"

"For a race at San Luis Speedway. I've only got about ten days to rebuild Bud's engine."

"There's always such a rush to do everything but your schoolwork, isn't there?"

"I'll do it," Cotton repeated.

"I hope so. Because if you flunk anything, there'll be no more racing until you bring your grades up, and you're riding a couple of *D*'s right now."

It was midnight when they wearily dropped their wrenches. Cotton used his father's car to drive Bud to the bus stop. He tried to read a schoolbook after he had taken a hot bath and slipped into bed. In five minutes he was asleep.

He awoke in the morning with a vague uneasiness plucking at his sleeve. His schoolbook was lying where he had dropped it. He frowned in pained recollection. *Walden*, the book was called, the journal of some old birdwatcher who had spent most of his time by a pond recording what he spent for nails and candles. Cotton had a quiz coming up today on the first twenty pages. While he was dressing, he tried to skim a few paragraphs, but his head felt as though it were stuffed with rags. He was still tired and stiff from last night.

The quiz was brutal. He struggled with a few questions, then grew resentful and began putting down terse guesses and leaving blanks.

After school he spoke to the shop instructor about using the equipment to turn down Bud's flywheel.

"Sure, if you want to clean up your mess," the instructor said. "Don't take it lightly that I'm letting you do it, either," he added. "There aren't six boys in this school I'd trust that far."

Cotton thanked him. He had one *A* coming up, at least. If they'd let him pick his own subjects, he could take home straight *A*'s.

He brought the flywheel to school the next day wrapped in a newspaper. It weighed eighteen pounds—full standard—and he intended to turn it down to eleven. Below that the risk arose of its flying apart at high speed. He worked on it after school until the custodian came to lock up.

As he walked up his street that evening, he realized he had left his Civics text in his locker. He halted, with a feeling of cold shock, remembering that his examination was tomorrow! He turned to run back; but, looking at his watch, he knew it was too late. Everything would be locked up. With relief, he recalled that he had study hall in the morning. He would have nearly an hour to cram.

Bud arrived after dinner, striding up the walk with a distinctive bounce, as though he had springs in his heels. He vibrated with energy.

"Where do we start, Chief?" he asked.

Cotton put him to work reassembling the engine in the yellow car, which would be Cotton's while the partnership lasted. Using a hone, Cotton began enlarging the cylinders of the other engine.

While they worked, they talked. Garage talk: a sentence or two, then silence. A little hammer-pounding. Conversation about Jimmy-blowers and oversize this-and-that.

Sometimes it wasn't about cars.

"I could run that body shop better than the boss does," Bud told Cotton. "The joker's never around. Buckets of paint go out the back door for jobs the guys do in their garages, and the men get sloppy. Of course, it's not easy as it looks to make a shop pay. You've got to know how to set up your books and figure a job. That's why I'm taking business courses."

Later, through the dark and silent town, Cotton drove him to the bus stop. A canopy of sea mist overhung the camphor trees. Driving back, he felt the cold claws of guilt on his skin. Finals! The very feel and smell of books made him go thick-witted and resentful. The timing couldn't have been worse, with the big racing season so close; for summer would come quickly, and tracks everywhere would be roaring. There would be no time to start working the bugs out of the car, with the season on. But school officials did not consult track promoters when they scheduled examinations.

His Civics final was a disaster.

He was not sure whether the secret ballot was a story by Nathaniel Hawthorne, or a Communist plot. "*Check whether True or False!*" Someone whispered: "They're all False!" He started checking them that way, but suddenly realized the original false statement was that *all* the statements were False. In fact, he suspected they might all be True. But now it was too late to change the answers that he had already put down on the paper.

He had answered only two-thirds of the questions when the bell rang.

Saturday came and he was working on the yellow and black car at dawn. At noon Bud arrived and they labored through the afternoon with a single break. Time was beginning to crowd them. A week from tomorrow they raced—if they had a car. Meantime, they must get the yellow car out of the way, then go on to the more demanding work of assembling the racing car.

At last the yellow roadster—Cotton's car, now—was complete, and they began the painstaking chore of putting the speedster together. Everything had to be closely "miked up"—measured to micrometer tolerances smaller than the thickness of a sheet of paper. When the engine was resting on its mounts, there would come the tasks of adjusting the springs to the weight of the new power plant, trying it out, and making endless final adjustments.

On Thursday afternoon they tightened the last bolt.

It was five-thirty and the light was fading. But there was no question of putting off the tryout until tomorrow. While Bud stood back, Cotton started the engine. The exhausts made a deep, watery burble. Cotton moved over and beckoned to Bud.

"Take the wheel! Let's try it out—"

The drag strip east of town was a mere alley of blacktop cut through the tall dry chaparral, its smooth surface striped by long slashes of burned rubber. Cotton checked the wheel lugs for safety, inspected the steering mechanism, and stood back. With a nervous grin, he gestured that it was ready to roll. He had seen more than one engine fly apart the first time it was called on for full power. *Seen* them! He had built them, breathed life into them—and taken them home in a washtub.

Bud kicked the starter and rocked the accelerator. The up-and-down kettledrumming throbbed in Cotton's body. Bud roared off down the strip. He braked, then sprinted again, traveling to the end of the asphalt in a series of rushes. Finally he did a U-turn and headed back.

Cotton waited in the cold evening wind, his hands thrust under his armpits for warmth. Bud parked and walked around the car thoughtfully. Cotton had seen experienced horsemen look at horses the same way. He was suddenly anxious.

"What's wrong?" he asked.

"I don't know," Bud said uneasily. "It bogs down when you gun it—"

"I'll check," Cotton muttered.

He drove to the end of the strip. Then, with a single tool—a dollar screwdriver—he made a thousand-dollar change in the timing. The carburetors weren't quite matched up, but they could wait. He recapped the distributor and drove back in a chain of swift starts and stops.

"Try it again," he told Bud.

He could see the dark head snap back as the car took off. This time Bud kept the throttle open all the way. A prolonged, rising shriek of power echoed back through the hills. When he returned, he looked at Cotton admiringly.

"You've got the touch," he said. "What'll we buy with that purse we're going to win Sunday?"

"A magnesium flywheel," replied Cotton, without hesitation.

But on Friday, the whole thing blew up.

Little buff-colored envelopes were passed out in his first-period class. They contained quarterly report cards. Sick with apprehension, Cotton opened his envelope. He gazed dully at an *F* in Civics and a *D* in English. *No more racing until you bring your grades up,* his father had said. He knew all too well that he meant it. San Luis was off; maybe the whole season was off. He put the envelope in his book and spent the rest of the day doodling pictures of racing cars.

CHAPTER 11 GUILTY AS CHARGED

In his room that night, Cotton pulled on a sweatshirt and angrily headed out of the house. The obligatory scene had been played; his father had not yielded an inch. The curtain had descended when Cotton said,

"I might as well join the Marines, if I've got to serve under a drill instructor!"

His parents had laughed. "Barbara," his father had said, "I don't believe you saluted when I came into the house tonight, did you?"

Cotton walked out on their laughter.

Outside, he was surprised to find that a heavy sea

fog had rolled in from the ocean, blanketing the town in its damp insulation. His heart was pounding, his mouth dry with anger. Big joke! He had been grounded until the next report cards came out. Tight-lipped and desperate, Cotton walked downtown. From a drugstore telephone booth, he called Bud and gave him the news. The lined hummed vacantly while Bud recovered from the shock.

"Oh, man!" he groaned, at last. "This is gonna hurt us. Did you reason with him?"

"Ha, ha, ha!" Cotton laughed. "Reason with *my* old man?"

"Can't you go up and watch me drive?"

"I can't even breathe the fumes; period."

"I could go up alone, I guess—"

"And the wagon'll be out of tune before you finish qualifying. If the weight has to be changed, you'll crank the wedge out instead of in, and go around on two wheels.—We're out of business, that's all."

A car passed the drugstore, its headlights woolly yellow orbs in the mist. All Cotton's worries, failures, and frustrations tangled in a hopeless knot in his mind. The fog outside seemed to enter through his eyes and blur his thinking. What he resented most was the unfairness of punishing him because he was weak in subjects he would never need anyway. Did a mechanical engineer need to know who the Lake Poets were?

Okay: if it was unfair, why not do something about it?

"Maybe if I went up with you once," he said slowly, "we could get it more or less set up. Then you could handle it alone for a while, or get somebody in the pits to help you—"

"Mmm." Bud sounded dubious.

In Cotton's mind, excitement began to stir. "Look, how about going to the Museum of Man with me Sunday morning?" he said.

"What for? Is there going to be a race in the parking lot?"

"No, but if we get tired of mummies and stuff, we can drive up to San Luis—"

Bud hesitated. "Oh—like that. Don't think I would, if I were you. No telling what your C.O. would do."

"Nothing's going to happen," Cotton said. "Just this once, and he won't even know."

Bud sounded apprehensive. "Even if he doesn't, you'll feel so guilty you won't enjoy it. After all, your old man's paying the bills."

"Guilty about what?" Cotton retorted. "I'm paying the bills on the car, aren't I? See you Sunday—Museum of Man."

On Saturday he stowed his pit clothes in the trunk of the car, along with all the tools and parts they might need. Sunday morning he dressed in a jacket and slacks.

"Guess I'll wheel down to San Diego," he told his mother. His father was working in the back yard.

"Fine. Anywhere in particular?"

"I'll cruise around the park for a while. Maybe I'll drop in at the Museum of Man. I hear they've got some new dinosaur bones. A mechanic can't know too much about dinosaurs."

His mother took him by the shoulders and made him look at her. Six inches shorter than he, she was dark-eyed and pretty and looked a little tired.

"Honey, I'm sorry. We want you to be happy more than we want anything in the world. But Dad is right. The only way to learn anything is to—well, get hurt a little."

Cotton put his hand over his heart. "And I'm really hurtin', Mom."

She laughed and kissed him. "Steak and potatoes tonight. Don't be late."

Driving down Coast Highway, Cotton was gloomy. But the instant he saw that little hand-carved ruby sparkling in the sun before the Museum of Man, he knew it was worth the risk.

By eleven o'clock, they had a spot in the pits.

The stands were filling slowly. Perhaps, Cotton thought, Al Stubbings had miscalculated the racing crowd's interest in his track's first anniversary. There was a fifty-lap race up north at Ascot today, and why should people drive so far to see this race when they could take one in right in Los Angeles? The big purse he had promised, based on a percentage of the gate, began to shrink like a pair of boiled socks.

Red Hasty stopped by to watch them tinker with the engine. Surprised, Cotton saw that he was wearing the uniform of the Stubbings-Mako team—peppermint-striped sport shirt and white pants. With condescending good nature, the redhead laid his hand on Bud's shoulder.

"Sorry I sounded off last time, Champ," he said. "No hard feelings?"

Bud winked at Cotton. "Not when we win. Did you take your practice laps with Mako's sprinter last week?"

Red wagged his head. "Ever ride a cannonball? That's what it's like. Just pull the trigger and hang on."

Cotton looked at his team shirt. "You're pretty thick with the Old Pro, for a punk kid," he joked.

Red tried not to look indecently proud. "Don't spread it around, but I may drive that car today! He said I looked so good on my practice laps that he'd like me to try it."

"I thought Earl Fallon drove the car regularly," Bud said.

"He does, but his wife wants him to quit. They've got a baby now, and she heard a rumor that racing is dangerous. So if Earl doesn't drive today, I'll get a chance at it."

Cotton looked around the pits. "I thought I saw Earl a few minutes ago." He owned up to a secret hope that Red wouldn't be launched in his sprint-car career before Bud was.

"Earl's here," Red admitted, "but he hasn't said for sure whether he'll drive."

Bud shook his hand, showing a more sincere good nature than Cotton could have mustered. "I hope he doesn't," he said. "Take my advice and don't have any babies, Red. It'd be the end of a great career."

Red chuckled, and Cotton relaxed and wished him luck, too. He was surprised to find that he meant it. If Bud couldn't have the break, then he was glad that it was happening to a friend.

Bud made the lineup for the fast roadster heat.

Watching him drive, Cotton was filled with pride. Car control was instinctive with Bud. His courage was more than mere rashness. It grew out of his absolute confidence and tactical ability. He faked and squirmed through the tangle like a slippery quarterback.

In the back of Cotton's mind lurked a ghost of guilt. He had never really lied to his parents before. Little things, perhaps, but never a deliberate breaking of the rules. This race was something he had stolen, and remorse embittered the taste of it.

On the ninth lap, smoke suddenly burst from Bud's car in a black cloud. The car faltered and started to spin. He regained control, but explosions broke the high hum of its power. He headed into the infield and stopped. Cotton ran over, listened, and gestured quickly. Bud cut the engine.

"Did I push it too hard?"

Cotton regarded the car gloomily. "No. I think I had the spark set up too far. We burned a valve."

"How are we going to get it home?"

"Tow it." Cotton was juggling the hazards. There was more than mere disappointment involved. "We'll have to sneak it into my garage as if nothing happened. If they catch me grinding in the new valve, I'll say it needs tuning up, or—or something."

"Lots of luck," Bud said.

They put the car back in highway trim, bolting on the fenders, running boards, and windshield.

Track officials announced that a change had been made in the starting lineup of the semi-main: Merle "Red" Hasty would drive the Braggan Special instead of Earl Fallon. They stayed to watch Red drive the purple and white car. The redhead hit the turns as if they were mortal enemies. He blistered the straightaways. He made Cotton think of a man teetering along the parapet of a ten-story building, half afraid he would not fall.

"You know where you usually see a driver like Red?" Bud said thoughtfully. "At carnivals—driving a motorcycle upside-down inside a cage."

Red placed third, and the second-place man knew he had been there. Red had practically worn out his rear standoff bars.

"How did you like the Museum of Man?" Cotton's father asked him that night. Cotton was lying on the sofa in the family room, reading *Speed Age*, while his mother put away the dinner things.

"Pretty good," Cotton mumbled.

Dr. Clark sat at a coffee table dealing a hand of solitaire. "What did you like best?"

"Huh? Oh—the dioramas, I guess. The Indian villages." Cotton was chilled with a feeling of sick apprehension. He was the world's worst liar; couldn't stand the suspense.

"I see you traded cars with Bud. Are you breaking up the partnership?"

"No. It needs a little work." Then he took a breath, laid his magazine on his stomach, and said: "We went up to the speedway."

"I was wondering. Did you enter your car?"

"Yes, sir."

Cotton's mother walked silently from the sink into the

family room and sat down. She sat there in silence.

"Cotton," asked his father, "what do you think I should do?"

Cotton tried to work up a feeling of persecution, but he only felt guilty. "I don't know."

"No opinion at all?"

Cotton sat up. He frowned at his feet and sighed heavily. "Ever since Coach Mooney crossed me up, things have gone sour."

"You mean you wouldn't have flunked Civics if it hadn't been for him?"

Cotton shrugged. "I don't know."

"You seem to have this curious idea that some mysterious force is out to make life difficult for you," his father observed.

"Everything was going okay till Mooney butted in. And now you seem to be waiting for me to blossom out as an executive type, or something."

"No one's said anything like that," his mother protested.

"Well, that's what you're thinking."

"Personally," said Dr. Clark, "I'm not thinking that far ahead. Do you want to know what I *am* thinking?"

Cotton looked at him, his eyes glazed with apprehension.

"That you'll have to sell your car," said the doctor.

"*Sell* it!"

"What did you expect? What answer could I possibly make to such utter disregard of the rules?"

Cotton felt as if he were being buried alive. "How am I supposed to get around?" he asked.

"How did you get around before you went car crazy? On your bicycle."

"Bicycle!" Cotton said, out of the deep well of his bitterness.

"Do you know some boy who wants to buy it?"

"No. It's half Bud's, anyway. For crying out loud, Dad—!"

"Then Bud will get half the money."

"You can't sell a hot rod like any old secondhand car! It's a 'thirty-two Ford, as far as the dealers' Blue Book goes. No value at all."

"I'll leave it at a used car lot on consignment, then. We'll find a buyer. I'll make it up to Bud if he loses anything on the sale."

Cotton stood up, trembling. "What if I won't sign the pink slip?"

His father peered at him sharply. "Settle down. You're white as a sheet. Don't let your adrenal glands run away with you."

From the way his heart was pounding, Cotton knew his glands were indeed churning out enough adrenalin for a combat situation. His mouth was plaster-dry.

"Why can't you put the car in storage?" he argued.

"A suspended sentence, you mean? No deal."

Cotton's mother rubbed her forehead, looking deeply troubled. "Dad, I don't know— Aren't you being a little hard on him?"

The doctor's palm smacked the coffee table. "Barbara, there is *no* easy way to learn *anything*! He's going to give up this whole ridiculous business until he settles down. *Then* we can talk about a deal."

Through a painful lump in his throat, Cotton choked: "That's a rotten way to—"

His father's face hardened dangerously, and Cotton looked down, kicked the magazine, and left the room. In his bedroom, he lay on the bed staring at the ceiling. After a few minutes he got up, pulled on his mechanic's overalls, and went to the garage. He removed a cylinder head of the car and inspected the burned valve. Nothing too serious. Nothing that could not be analyzed and made right. As he worked, his nerves began to ease out. That was what was so great about mechanical work: you knew for sure when you had done a good job. You knew when it was finished.

What would he do when he no longer had a car to work on? I'll go nuts, he thought. It wasn't merely a car his father had told him to get rid of. It was the only part of his life he could control.

CHAPTER 12 BIG FRIDAY

When Cotton awoke the next morning, fat drops of rain were pelting the roof and blowing against the windows like handfuls of birdshot. Out-of-focus sheets of water slithered down the glass. Leaves clawed against the screens as the wind bowed the shrubs. It reminded him that he had left a window open above the workbench when he quit last night. He dressed quickly, put a slicker over his head, and tramped out to the garage. He switched on the light. Then he froze, his hand still on the switch.

The roadster was gone.

Stunned, he stared around the empty floor, still littered with junk left from the rebuilding. With a groan of despair he turned and ran to the house. His mother was turning bacon in a frying pan.

"Where's my car?" he demanded.

"I don't know. Get ready for breakfast, now. We'll talk about it later."

"Did he take it to a used car lot?"

"Yes, but I don't know where. I won't talk about it."

"He's crazy! They'll sell it for about three hundred dollars. The crankshaft and cam are worth that. Mom, I've got thousands of hours in that car—"

His mother shook her head and came to him.

"I know, son—I know so well. But we've got thousands of hours in you, too, and we're not going to see them spoiled by a red hot rod. Don't you understand? You've *got* to buckle down to work! It won't kill you to forget about cars until summer."

"I told him he could store it!" Cotton backed away when she tried to put her arms around him.

"Dad gave you a chance before, but you broke your word. That's why he decided something drastic was necessary to wake you up."

Cotton went to his room, heavy with despair and bitterness. As he ran his electric shaver over his jaws, he stared at himself in the mirror. His face was white and tense; he forced the despair from his eyes and worked at an expression of stony indifference. By the time he had finished shaving, he had achieved a cynical look which he decided would do to meet the world with.

He walked to school, refusing to think of riding his old bicycle. He would as soon have ridden a tricycle.

Only a dozen other students were in the study hall when he sauntered in and dropped his books noisily on his desk. The teacher glanced up, frowned, and because it was not quite nine o'clock said nothing. Red Hasty was one of the students in the hall. He could not wait for Cotton to get settled before hurrying over to lean on his desk.

"Are you crazy?" he whispered. "Paul Dobson says he saw your car on a used car lot on the way to school!"

Cotton flipped a book open and leaned back, grinning. "My old man thinks I ought to trade it in on a rickshaw—something I can make money with."

"Come on—what's the story?" Red demanded.

"Little domestic crisis. Did they have a price on it?"

"Asking four hundred. Dobson's going to try to buy it."

Cotton rubbed his knuckles into his palm. "Tell him there's a bonus if he acts fast. A knuckle sandwich."

Red nodded. "I'll pass the word. You're not giving up racing, are you?"

Cotton flipped the pages of the book. "Nah. It'll blow over."

Red snapped his fingers. "Hey, listen! Why not drive over to the Phoenix races with me this week end?"

"It's just sprints, isn't it?"

Red's face broke into a big grin. "Right. I'm driving that old box of Mako's again! Earl Fallon's quit the team. I may get to drive steady."

"Great. Take it easy and don't try to set any records, though. When did you turn twenty-one?" he asked, with a wink.

Red lowered his voice. "Gil's going to fix me up with some papers. I don't know how long I'll last, but he seems to like the way I handle a car. But there's something else, too. The car's in the barn, you know, as far as Gil's concerned. Any kicks he gets out of driving now, he'll have to get from the pits. Like an old boxer teaching a young one the tricks. You know?"

Cotton nodded gravely. "You looked good out there the other day, too. Nobody will ever call you chicken, boy. But if you're going to Phoenix, don't forget what Herb Jacobs always says: 'Drive as fast as you want, but don't drive over your head.' "

Red chuckled. "You're liable to hear anything in a junk yard," he said.

All day it rained. Cotton's spirits drooped like the rattling fans of the palm trees on the school lawn. He felt joyless and hollowed-out; nothing seemed to have any importance. After dinner, he said:

"I guess I'll go to a show."

"All right, dear," Cotton's mother said. "I'll drive you down."

"No homework?" asked the doctor.

"No. I did it this afternoon. Like you said," Cotton added.

His father turned a page of his newspaper. "Fine," he said drily.

The irony in his voice stung Cotton. Okay—that's it! he thought bitterly. If you don't like what happens, don't blame me . . . .

At the theater, he consulted the card which told him when he would get out. Then he turned and peered south toward Guarantee Ford's used car lot. The highway's black glass reflected the colored lights of stores and autos.

While he was in the theater the sky cleared. He came out to a cold darkness with sparse traffic and lonely street lights. Hands in his pockets, arms pulled close to his ribs, he walked to the used car lot. The sales shack was closed, but strings of powerful lights burned above the rows of cars. Fat droplets of rain sparkled on their waxed surfaces. His own car stood in the front rank, right on the sidewalk, with the price splashed across the windshield.

$400 ! ! ! Loaded ! ! !

Cotton glanced furtively around the lot. He was afraid to stand too close to the cars for fear of bringing a watchman. On the other hand, part of what he wanted to find out was whether there *was* a watchman. He sauntered to the roadster and kicked a front tire like a prospective customer. (If the car didn't collapse, it was presumed to be roadworthy.) The white canvas top was raised and the doors were locked.

He drifted aimlessly about the lot for a while. No one bothered him. He decided there was no watchman on duty. Probably at ten o'clock a junior salesman would come back to turn out the lights.

He walked back to the business district and telephoned his mother to pick him up.

After school the next day—Tuesday—he sorted through his extra parts, selected what was most salable, and put it in a carton. He got Red to drive him to an auto supply store which carried a line of new and used racing parts—a speed shop, they called it. A speedy place to get rid of money, too, though not nearly so fast to pick it up.

"What's the idea?" Red asked him, as Cotton got the carton out of the trunk. "George won't give you twenty cents on the dollar for that stuff. You can probably use most of it sooner or later."

"Sooner's the way I need money," Cotton said. He carried the carton inside and deposited it on the scratched glass counter. George Coggan, the owner, sauntered up and looked into the box. "Make an offer," Cotton said.

Coggan shrugged. "I can't give you what the stuff's worth, Cotton. Why don't you sell one or two parts, if you need cash?"

"I'm going out of the racing business for a while," Cotton told him.

"That's terrible!" Coggan said. "How am I going to make a living if you kids all go stock?"

While Coggan figured up what the parts were worth, Cotton read the posters on the wall. The Phoenix race was advertised on a big black and white placard showing two sprint cars skidding through a turn. He could smell the hot oil and nitromethane; he trembled to the shaking roar of the exhausts.

George Coggan was generous with his apologies as he counted out forty-three dollars for equipment which had cost over a hundred.

On Thursday, Cotton drew out all but a dollar of his

savings account at the bank. Added to what Coggan had paid him, he had nearly seventy-five dollars. He walked down to the used car lot again, fearful that the car might have been sold since yesterday. He looked for the cheerful ruby gleam of it in the line and a quick pain seized him.

The roadster was gone.

He stared at the gap it had occupied in the line of used automobiles. He was struck cold and nerveless by the knowledge that it had been sold.

Then hope rallied. Perhaps a customer was just trying it out—

He walked onto the lot and inspected other cars until a big, balding man with horn-rimmed glasses sauntered from the sales shack. The salesman took a cigar from his mouth, picked a piece of wet tobacco leaf from his lip, and asked,

"Something for you, young fella?"

"Just looking around," Cotton said.

"Sure, take your time."

"Didn't you have a red Deuce—'thirty-two Ford, I mean?"

"We still got it—it's at the car-wash. We're having the chrome rustproofed. Don't take long to pit, in this climate."

"It was already—" Cotton began, and bit his tongue.

"How's that?" The heavy crescent eyebrows went up behind the glasses.

"It looked like it was already rustproofed. I was looking it over yesterday."

"Yeah. Well, we wanted to be sure. Nothing's too

good for our customers." The salesman grinned, chewed on the cigar, and sauntered away at a flatfooted waddle.

Friday.

He got a real break that afternoon. His mother was away when he got home from school. A note explained that she had gone to San Diego. He threw some clothing in an old suitcase and stowed it, his sleeping bag, and some other odds and ends in the garage. He found some of his old Boy Scout camping equipment and put it with the other gear. Then he moved everything around to the side of the garage by the trash barrels. Emptying the wastebaskets was one of his duties, so there was little chance that anyone would discover the things. From the desk in his room, he searched out his extra set of keys for the car.

It was time to move. His mother, if she ran true to form, would come hurrying in about six and start banging pans around. It was now five-thirty. Cotton scribbled a note and left it on the kitchen table.

Gone to San Diego on the bus. Bud and I are going to a show. Don't wait up.

For an instant, as he was leaving, he hesitated by the door. He wished he could say, *Don't worry*; but that might tip them off.

Then he wrote another note, and left it instead.

Dear Mom and Dad: I thought I'd take the bus up to

Uncle Don's for the week end and come back Sunday night. I'm taking my books with me. Didn't want to ask because you might say NO. With warmest personal regards,

Robert "Cotton" Clark

He had picked up the phrase, "warmest personal regards," from a junk-mail advertisement. By joking it up a little, he could be fairly sure they wouldn't get suspicious and call Uncle Don, in Bakersfield, to learn whether he had really gone there.

He left the house almost on a run.

He was one of the early dinner customers at Natalie's Café, where he ordered a cheeseburger, malt, and a piece of boysenberry pie. A tingling like internal gooseflesh kept him on edge. He killed time reading a newspaper and drinking coffee until ten to seven, when the theater opened. Then he strode down the darkening main street with its booming diesel traffic and bought a ticket.

At nine-thirty he left the theater. As he gazed down the highway toward the Guarantee lot, he could feel the tendons in the back of his neck tighten. He strolled a block closer and saw that there were still customers on the lot. To kill time, he turned down a side street and walked to the cliffs above the ocean. He sat on the ground and listened to the steady washing of the waves below. It was too dark to see them, but he made out the lights of a ship out where the sky came down to the horizon. Already he felt as though there were a great distance between himself and his home. The sound of the ocean, the darkness and the emptiness folded about him with a choking sadness. He got up, walked back to the middle of town, and returned to the used car lot.

The lot was closed now. To his relief, the strings of lights were dark. For a few minutes he sat on a bus bench, watching the lot. The sales shack was dark. No one was in sight. He walked quickly to his car and tried the door. It was locked. He unlocked the door and slipped in, twisted the ignition lock and kicked the starter. The engine hit instantly. The power of it eased into him, smoothing the rough edges of his anxiety.

He drove to his street and parked below the house. Walking quickly, he went down the side yard to the trash barrels. There was too much gear to carry in one trip. He carried what he could, went back for the rest, and was just placing his sleeping bag on his shoulder when a voice said:

"Good evening!"

Cotton jumped. There, across the low grapestake fence, stood a man in the next yard!

"What are you doing?"

Cotton recognized the voice: it was Mr. Huffner, their neighbor on the west.

"Oh, hello, Mr. Huffner," he said. "It's Cotton. I was just moving some junk out of here."

". . . I see. Heard you padding around. I hear you're selling your car," he said.

"Yes."

"I daresay things will be quieter around here for a while," the neighbor said. "Without that engine blasting the shingles off my house."

"Should be real quiet," Cotton said. "Good night."

Reaching the car, he threw the sleeping bag into the back and took off.

"Hi. This's Cotton."

He stood in an outside telephone booth at a drive-in hamburger stand in East San Diego. It was a few minutes past eleven. He had been driving a half-hour.

Bud's voice was rough with sleep. "Call me late some time, Champ. I'm only putting in an eighteen-hour day, going to college and holding a job."

"I had to call you, and this is the first time I've had a chance."

Something in his tone woke Bud quickly. "What's up?" he asked.

"I'm heading for Phoenix."

"Phoenix! In what?"

Cotton had told him about the car disaster; they had even discussed the matter of how the money should be divided when the car was sold.

"I borrowed my car for a few days," he said. "I'm going to take in the races this week end. Then I'll probably hang around Phoenix for a few days."

"What's the idea?" Bud demanded. He sounded disgruntled.

"The idea is that this town turns my stomach. If I

have to give up cars to finish school, then I'll give up school and get back to cars. I'm eighteen. They can't make me finish."

"You're nuts. What do you want to be, a crop picker? You won't even make that, if they pick you up for car theft."

"It's not car theft—I haven't signed the pink slip."

"I hope you know the rules. The lot will report it stolen when it shows up missing in the morning, and it'll be your neck if you're wrong."

"They'll check with my folks first, and I left a letter. So the word probably won't go out until Monday, because they think I'm coming back. And by that time I'll be out of state."

"You're going to a lot of trouble to be a teen-age dropout, aren't you?"

"I'll explain it when I see you," Cotton said. "Why don't you drive over to Phoenix tomorrow? I'll give you the story then."

Bud hesitated. There was a different note in his voice when he spoke again.

"I guess I can make it. I'll have to work a couple of hours, but I'll be there before dark. Where'll I find you?"

"I'm going to get a room in a motel, but I'll be at the pits till they close the track. If you aren't there by dark, I'll hang around outside."

CHAPTER 13 HOODOO WAGON

Cotton drove another hour. Highway 80, the main route east to the desert and Arizona, climbed through oak and chaparral to the sparse pine country of the mountains. It grew cold—the altitude was five thousand feet now—and he turned on the heater. At Pine Valley, a resort community in a mountain meadow, he stopped at a restaurant which was about to close for the night. He got a hamburger and a glass of milk. Afterward, he took a side road which followed the edge of a meadow.

Near the north end of the meadow was a cluster of giant oaks overspreading huge boulders. In the middle of these boulders was a sheltered space in which he could park without being seen by roving highway patrolmen. He drove across the rough ground into the miniature campground, inflated his air mattress and spread his sleeping bag on the ground. It was midnight, and he wanted to be up early. He crawled into his blankets.

Suddenly he was aware of the silence. It was huge—no rumble of traffic, no Navy jets roaring across the sky; just a big vacancy which made him tingle. He felt a sense of excitement, which was not quite fear, at what he was doing. Gazing at the black sky, he saw how white the stars were. He filled his lungs with the crisp mountain air, sighed, and turned over to sleep.

The sun woke him early. He drove back to the village and shaved in a service station rest room. After a trucker's breakfast in the little restaurant—sausage, buckwheat cakes, a jug of syrup, and scrambled eggs—he headed up the highway.

It was still early when he crossed the summit and plunged down the winding drop into the gray lifelessness of the desert. At the bottom the altitude was only about two thousand feet; it was hot here. As the road unkinked, it was possible to see for miles in all directions. He shoved at the gas pedal and was doing a hundred in a matter of seconds. With that out of his system, he grinned, slowed down to sixty-five, and held it there.

Shortly before noon, with the Colorado River and the great wastelands of the desert behind him, he reached

Phoenix. He got a room in a little stucco motel, carried his things inside, and headed for the fairgrounds.

It seemed odd to go into the pits without a car. After getting his pit pass, he roamed into the sunburned, noisy world of the big sprint cars. Drivers in gleaming sprinters were out on the track, charging and sliding, getting the feel of the surface. From now until race time tomorrow, gear ratios would be changed back and forth, dozens of tires experimented with, engines worked over.

A yellow car, low as a crab and wide, shot by him—the A. K. Briggs Special, Billy Michaels' car. It was Michaels' except that the Briggs Manufacturing Company owned it and two or three others like it, which moved about the country competing in all the important races. Michaels had been runner-up in a national points race a couple of years ago. Another car boomed past, a red and gold machine Cotton did not recognize. Its engine was backfiring, and the driver pulled into the pits.

Cotton roamed around for a half-hour, watching the teams of mechanics work on the cars. The sun blazed down with dry ferocity. Nearly everyone was in a tee shirt. From the back turn, he heard the bone-shaking roar of a sprinter going for the wall. Tingling, he turned to watch it; it sounded hotter than a jet. The car was a robin's-egg blue, wide and flat—another car he did not know. As it rolled from the track, he followed it through the pits until it stopped. A mechanic in white pants and a peppermint-striped shirt spoke to the driver.

The mechanic looked familiar—the shirt was unmistakable. Cotton recognized Charlie Grimes, Mako's ace troubleshooter. It must be a new Stubbings and Mako car! They already had three cars operating; a new one probably meant an old one was being retired, unless they had the price of another driver and crew.

"How's that blue heater look to you?" a man said, behind him.

Cotton turned. The man was about fifty, and huge—he looked like a fullback from the old Flying Wedge days. He wore a gray suit and a red tie, and had once had red hair, though it had gone almost completely gray. His hair was cropped short, and his eyebrows were clipped. He had blunt, friendly features, and was smiling at Cotton as though he knew him. Cotton had never seen him before.

"Uh—the blue car?" he faltered.

"Yes."

"It looks pretty good," Cotton said. "Do you know it?"

"No, but I know you," the man said. "You're Cotton Clark."

Cotton's stomach dropped. *He's a juvenile officer!* he thought. His folks must have reported him missing! Taking a closer look at the man, he was *certain* he was an officer—he had the look. His head was shaped like a brick, straight up the back, and his nose seemed to have been flattened in a brawl.

Cotton cleared his throat. "Yeah, that's me," he said.

"A friend of yours asked me to say hello," the man said. "Bud Smith. Know him?"

"Sure, I know him! He—" He was about to say that Bud was coming over, but decided he had better not. He might involve Bud, too.

"My name's R. C. Cunningham," the big man said.

Cunningham—a small bell rang in his mind. "Do you make speed equipment?" Cotton asked quickly.

The man smiled. "Say, you *are* a racing fan, if you've heard of *me*. Unless Bud told you."

"I didn't tell him," Bud's voice said. Cotton looked around, bewildered, and finally saw Bud sitting on a jeep can beside a car twenty feet away. Bud began to laugh as he got up and came to join them.

The tension ran out of Cotton. "The heck you didn't," he said. "Mr. Cunningham was your shop teacher, and he makes front ends for sixty dollars."

"Very good," said Mr. Cunningham. He offered his hand, which was about the size of a frying pan, and Cotton took it. "I've got equipment on some of the cars here," he explained, "so I thought I'd drive over with Bud and watch them perform."

Cotton nodded toward the blue speedster in Mako's slot. "How did *you* like the blue sprinter?" he asked him.

"Very nice. But I have no equipment on it, so I can't waste time discussing the car. I'll leave you and Bud to figure it out, and I'll see you later."

With a wave of the hand, he moved off through the jungle of cars and equipment.

"Where are you staying?" Bud asked.

"I'm in a motel out on the highway. We'll get them to move a cot in for you."

"Okay. Let's get something to drink."

Through the oppressive heat they walked to a drink stand. There was no shade, but they sat on a bench against a wall and managed to get their heads out of the sunlight.

"Hot," Cotton said.

"You might as well get in shape for detention camp," Bud said. "You'll get a lot of sunlight and fresh air up there. Building roads. Chauffeuring a wheelbarrow."

Cotton snorted. "How can you steal your own car?"

"I don't know, but I've got an idea you've just found a way."

Cotton slid down on the bench. "The way I feel about it is this. I could have done better in school last quarter than I did. Okay. I said I'd bring my grades up. The business about not racing was just—well, showing me he's running things."

"He is," Bud said tersely. "Get used to the idea."

"He's not running things where selling my car is concerned," Cotton retorted.

"That was rough, all right. But you asked for it."

Cotton's head turned. He stared at the other boy. "Hey, whose team are you on?"

"Neither," Bud said. "I just drive cars."

Cotton kept looking at him. Bud took a swallow of his drink and set the bottle on the bench. "I've got enough problems without getting involved in somebody else's. For instance, I'm involved in yours right now, and it could cost me plenty."

Cotton felt confused and resentful. "You mean about losing money on the car?"

"No. Mr. Cunningham asked me on the way over whether we'd changed the registration when we put my engine in your car. It's a misdemeanor not to. I guess I knew that, but I'd forgotten. Now we've got a stolen car floating around with my engine in it!"

"Is that my fault?" Cotton snapped.

"It's your fault if they've reported it stolen."

Cotton bit his lip. His anger was dissolving in guilt and a feeling of apprehension.

Bud finished his drink and stood up. "I know how you feel, and I guess I'd feel the same way. But the point is, I can't afford to get tied up with somebody who's living dangerously like you're starting out to. I figure things are dangerous enough in this business without stealing cars."

He suddenly grinned. "Come on—let's take a look at that car."

As they walked toward the track, Mako's old purple and white sprint car started up. It streaked down the straightaway, made the front turn, and headed through the back stretch. Cotton's mood was not improved any when he saw Red's gold helmet under the roll bar. He was going to drive it, all right.

A new sound pierced the baritone howling of the Offenhauser engines under the hoods of most of the racing cars: the nervous screech of a sports car. They turned to stare as a forest-green car, sleek and shining, came down the front chute. Bud turned to follow it through the turn.

"What's that thing doing here? It's no sprint car. They'll knock it right off the track."

Cotton felt a thrill of excitement. He had a secret admiration for the sports cars, which most racing people regarded as an affectation, like a silk hat and a monocle.

"He's got standoff bars on it," he pointed out. "I guess he's really going to run."

The car passed with the characteristic earsplitting whine of its breed. It was a Maserati—a car you could buy for a hundred and fifty thousand dollars a dozen (slightly more per unit in smaller quantities). Cotton liked their low, windswept lines and their versatility. But they did not belong on an ordinary speedway: that had been proved time and again. It was a bow and arrow against a cannon.

"The boys will love that color," commented Bud.

Cotton nodded. "Hoodoo wagon," he muttered. Green was supposed to be bad luck, like eating peanuts, or having women in the pits.

Over at the edge of the track, a man was doing deep knee bends. There was something familiar about his blocky figure and black oilcloth cap. Cotton smiled.

"See the guy doing the squats? That's Herb Jacobs. Maybe I told you about him. Herb runs a wrecking yard. He's helped me with every car I've built. I guess he's forgotten more about cars than Offenhauser ever knew. Come on over and meet him."

He introduced Bud to the wrecking yard entrepreneur and they sat on the ground to talk. Herb looked as pallid as ever, as though he had just spent a month lying under a car; but his naturalness and low-pressure amiability were relaxing.

"How come you're not working?" Cotton asked him.

"I got the rent paid, so I'm taking a day off. Also, I thought you might need a character witness in juvenile court."

Cotton winced. *Here it comes again!* he thought. Did everybody in California have to drive to Phoenix to tell him what a mistake he was making?

"Don't worry about me," he said.

Herb cocked a cynical eye at him. "Somebody's got to. Guess who called me in the middle of the night?"

There was a cold cramp of anxiety in Cotton's belly. "Who?"

"Your father."

"How come?"

"Somebody stole your car off the Guarantee lot. The police noticed an empty slot in the line of cars and called the owner. The owner checked and called your father. Your father checked and called me. I checked and here I am."

"Look, it's not theft if—"

Herb waved his hand impatiently. "Turn it off, I've heard the song before. You'd be surprised how many kids' folks decide to sell their car, and some joker is always telling me, 'I'm going to steal it back, Herb! It isn't theft if I own it, is it?' The answer is, yes: it's theft. Because your father signed a consignment slip when he left the car at the agency."

"But I own—"

"Uh-huh. And he owns you, Rover Boy, and as your trustee he can sign you into the burlap bag factory, if he feels like it. How are you going to get that car home, now?"

Cotton picked up a pebble and tossed it onto the track. "Let me worry about getting the car home."

"I'm going to do just that. As a matter of fact, I was coming over for the races anyway. I'm going to make one last speech: I've got a lot of time and parts tied up in you, and it begins to look like I was wasting them. I don't necessarily go along with what your father was doing, but when it comes to things like stealing cars, I vote the straight parental ticket. End of speech.—See that Maserati?" he said. "It shouldn't happen to a go-kart. What's going to happen to that car if he races?"

"Don't you like sports cars?" Bud asked him.

"Like a jeweler likes watches—only they ought to stay away from the ovals. They don't have the acceleration or the beef. Now, watch this blue wagon when he opens up after the turn—"

A sprint car was streaking down the track toward them.

It was the robin's-egg blue car Cotton had decided was Mako's. Some minor change had been made on it and the driver was testing it again. Conversation died while the stadium was filled with the giant thunder of its passing. Cotton stared as he saw a glint of metal where the white-helmeted driver's right hand should have been. Mako was driving. There was a deafening blast of power as it left the turn and opened up; it shot ahead like a toy car given a kick.

"Notice who was driving it?" Herb asked.

Cotton nodded. "Is he going to try to drive a hundred laps with that hook?"

"He's just setting it up, probably. Johnny Partmann's going to drive. He's signed up with Stubbings for the season. They must be paying him a fortune. He won the national championship not so long ago, and the Western States two years running."

They watched Mako take a couple of laps and head into the infield. Cotton stood up quickly. A dull anger lay in him like a stone. Bud and Herb were the two best friends he had, but even they didn't seem to understand the situation.

"Let's go over and listen to Mako blow about his new car," he said.

Herb walked beside him. "If you survive this week end," he said, "I'll talk to your father Monday night. Maybe I can make things clearer to him about how you feel. If you don't survive it, I'll send you a postcard in the detention home."

CHAPTER 14 RACE DAY

"I told Partmann to be here no later than ten," Gil Mako was saying, as they walked up. The big black-haired driver was sunburned and his face was an angry red. Frowning at the engine compartment as a couple of mechanics peered into it, he grumbled, "Give these hot-dog drivers a few wins, and they start acting like bullfighters. Next week I may have to furnish a satin bathrobe for him to walk to the car in."

Charlie Grimes pushed a hydraulic jack under the rear of the blue speedster. "Johnny'll be here," he said.

He jacked up the rear end, selected a socket wrench, and started removing bolts from the gear box.

Cotton swept his glance from one end of the car to the other. He heared Herb murmur, "Sweet!" Smoothly contoured as an oyster shell, the car hid its four hundred horsepower nicely. The top of the roll bar, the highest point, was less than three feet above the track. All the instrument dials were masked off except the speedometer. In small gold letters on the side was the driver's name: *Johnny Partmann.* Below the name was an emblem: *S-M Special.*

Herb couldn't keep his hands off the car. He trailed his fingers over the chromed ram tubes and smiled at Cotton. He could appreciate a fine car, even if he didn't like the owner.

"Look, would you mind—" Scowling, Mako raised his voice, and Herb dropped his hand. Mako gave him a sour grin. "As they say in kindergarten," he said, "*'We look with our eyes.'* Okay?"

"You're the boss," Herb said.

Cotton was embarrassed for him. Mako saw him then and gave him and Bud a salute. "Hi. Seen the redhead drive?" he asked, tilting his head toward the track, where Red was heading in.

Cotton glanced at Red's car. "He looks good," he said.

Red drove into the pits and climbed out, his face flushed. He appeared tense and nerved-up, but happy. "How's she feel to you?" Mako asked.

"Good. Maybe a little more weight up front. What do you think?"

"It's what *you* think," Mako said impatiently. "You're

the driver.—Change the wedge on this," he told one of the mechanics. "No, wait. Charlie, let that gear box go. Let's go over and have something to eat. You guys, too," he said to Cotton and Bud. Then, seeing that Herb seemed to be in their party, he added: "How about coming along?"

Herb rubbed his nose. "Thanks.—Herb Jacobs," he said, offering his hand.

Mako frowned. "Jacobs—Jacobs . . . . Didn't you use to drive?"

"Back in the wooden-wheel days," Herb said.

Mako chuckled and slapped him on the back. "Sure, sure! What have you been doing with yourself, Herb?"

"Running a junk yard," Herb said, frankly.

There was an embarrassed pause. "Well, great," said Mako with false enthusiasm.

"Junk yard, nothing!" Cotton protested. "He's got the best wrecking yard in the county. Where else can you buy points for a 1908 Autocar?"

They laughed, and started across the infield. One thing about racing people, Cotton thought: they might wrangle and criticize each other, but they had so much in common, underneath it all, that they got more fun out of being with enemies who loved cars than with friends who didn't.

They left the fairgrounds and entered a little café called the Log Cabin. The walls were paneled with knotty pine, and red gingham cloths brightened the tables. Mako picked a booth and had a table dragged up to extend their space. After they had ordered, he told the waitress,

"Give the check to me, Miss."

When Herb tried to argue, the Old Pro ended the argument with a gesture, and pulled out his cigarettes. He held the package with his good left hand and used his mechanical hand to draw out a cigarette, which he immediately dropped. Cotton heard him mutter something as he knocked the cigarette to the floor. He successfully drew out a second. Cotton felt suddenly guilty. He glanced at him with a sympathy he would not have expected to experience toward the old race track monarch. He sensed that a man like Mako could feel more crippled by the loss of a hand than a less competitive man might by the loss of a leg.

The conversation limped, handicapped by the fact that Mako, the host, was setting the pace but was saying nothing. The door opened and a young man in a red tee shirt and gray slacks entered. He wore driving gloves with half-fingers, and there was a well-groomed, almost affected look about him. Seeing him take a stool at the counter, Mako gave a snort.

"There's Fancy Dan, the sports car man," he said. "Didn't know they ate ordinary food, like earthlings."

Cotton glanced at the man, who was apparently the driver of the Maserati.

Red laughed. "It's gonna be National Disaster Day for him, if he qualifies in that crate."

Herb looked at the young man, and smiled. "He'd do better in a Porsche or Lotus," he said.

Mako's eye settled on him. "Why?"

"Better traction," said Herb. "Rear end engine."

"That the only reason he won't win?" Mako asked.

"There's lots of reasons," said Herb, " but that's one."

"Lemme tell you something," said Mako, laying his palm flat on the table. "No sports car will ever win at a regulation oval, because they aren't built for it. Plus, the drivers have to have teething biscuits, and feedings at regular intervals. They aren't drivers—they're ballet dancers in crash hats."

Bud looked up from his Coke. "They're as good as any U.S.A.C. driver," he said. "They drive wet or dry tracks, right and left turns, night or day."

"There ain't one of them," Mako retorted, "that can take a turn without riding the brake. Well, brother, you can't win races with your foot on the brake."

"They've got special problems," Cotton admitted. "But suppose you took one of those bugs and made some changes in it? Then maybe you'd have a chance."

"*What* changes?" said Mako.

It was Herb who answered. Something in the way he spoke told Cotton he had thought about this a great deal.

"Offset the engine to the left," he said. "Beef up the suspension. The car's five hundred pounds lighter to begin with, so you'd have less tire trouble and you wouldn't have to carry as much fuel."

"Why don't they do it, then?" Red challenged.

Mako rubbed out his cigarette. "Because by the time you've made all the modifications, you've got a one-purpose car again. You're right back where U.S. cars already are. Why fight it? We've already got the best racing car in the world. They tried it with two Ford-powered Lotuses at Indy, and how'd they come out? A plain old Brickyard roadster took the money."

Herb gave his mild smile. "They both finished—one of

'em in second place. Times are changing, Gil. Would you match your new wagon against a Lotus with a big horsepower engine?"

"I'd match it against a jet-powered Lotus running on railroad tracks!" Mako snapped back.

There was laughter at his vehemence. Their food came and the subject was dropped. Cotton had the impression that no one really wanted to carry the argument any further. Racing arguments were like disputes over religion and politics: no one ever proved anything, but everybody got mighty heated up.

Perhaps because of the discussion, Cotton watched with special interest every time the Maserati went out. It was a beautiful, functional car. It handled well, but in coming out of the corners it seemed to lack the jump of the big Offenhauser-powered sprinters. However, since the car was lighter and the brakes were more effective, the driver was able to hold the power on longer. It would be interesting to see how the little green car made out.

After dinner, Bud moved into the motel with Cotton. The streets were still hot, but an air conditioner made their room almost chilly. It seemed strange and exciting to be completely free, responsible to no one. I can lie on the bed without taking my shoes off, Cotton reflected; so he did. The small, clean room seemed lodged in a backwash in time. While he stayed here, he need not make up his mind about anything. Just drift.

He could have it like this all the time, he reflected, if he quit school and got a job. He had more education, right now, than a lot of top mechanics. On the other hand, he wanted at least to finish high school. What he *didn't* want was somebody on his back all the time, checking him in and out, peering into his textbooks to see how far he had read since yesterday.

They showered in the bright, tiled bathroom, crawled in bed, and talked till midnight. Bud asked no more questions about his plans.

In the morning, they watched Johnny Partmann take the blue S-M Special out and make it look easy to set the pole-winning time. You didn't need to show up early, if you could drive like Johnny, Cotton thought. There were a couple of minor wrecks, some spin-outs, and one car blew a piston on its qualifying lap. Red made the second heat of the main event.

In the bright, dusty air there was a throb of excitement. All the mechanics were sweating over their cars, while the drivers explained earnestly what they thought the engines needed to tease another mile per hour out of them. Every car here was in virtually perfect condition; yet in some there existed minute faults which a few minutes on the track would rip into great, destructive fractures. There were differences in the drivers, too; but everyone here thought that he had the combination of right driver and right engine. Envy twisted sharply in Cotton.

"How much do you think it would cost to build a sprinter?" he asked.

"Let's do something cheap this year," Bud replied. "Like buying a race horse."

"A lot of these guys don't have that kind of money," Cotton argued. "They pool their money and stop racing when they run out."

"That's where we are right now. We just ran out of money."

Cotton pointed out a white and red car with an exceptionally high profile. "Now, there's what I mean. That old rail job was probably born about 1936. It sat behind some garage for ten years, until somebody offered two hundred dollars for it, rust and all. They lowered it, got new wheels, shoved in a new engine—"

"—For five thousand dollars," Bud added. "I've been riding that same dream so long I know all the gas stations along the way."

"Don't be a defeatist. We could get a secondhand engine for fifteen hundred dollars."

Bud laughed wryly. "Now we've got an engine. But they're very fussy about contestants having a car, too."

"I think you're disgusting," Cotton said. "How did we get money for the rods we're driving now? By working."

"But a sprinter means three-dollar-an-hour work," Bud said.

Cotton knew he was right. Still . . ."Maybe they could use another man at your body shop," he said.

"When the boss needs another man, he just doubles up on somebody else's work," Bud told him.

"What about Mr. Cunningham? Doesn't he ever hire help?"

Bud shrugged. "Let's ask him."

They found the shop teacher with two men Cotton did not recognize. Mr. Cunningham was crouching beside a front wheel examining the suspension, while the other men inspected the engine. Mr. Cunningham glanced up at the boys and wiped sweat from his forehead.

"What's new?" he asked.

"Cotton's got a financial problem," Bud said. "He was wondering if you could use a hand in the machine shop."

Mr. Cunningham studied Cotton. "You're talking about a summer job?"

"Maybe steady. I graduate in June—with a little luck."

"Not going on to college?"

"I'm not sure . . . ."

"I may have some piecework later on. Nothing steady, though. I'm a pretty small operator." He turned his head and called to one of the men who were looking at the engine. "Jim, do you ever hire high school graduates at your plants?"

The man straightened and looked at Cotton. He wore a short-sleeved shirt, which was not unusual, but also a tie, which was. "Sometimes," he said. "Not many. And I'm afraid Detroit might be a long way for this lad to commute."

"What about your regular employee program? Are you hiring anybody without a college degree?"

The man winced. "In our plants, the guys that put paper cups in the water cooler have to have an A.B.!"

Mr. Cunningham gave Cotton a sympathetic smile. "That's from the engineer's mouth," he said. "Jim's a top man with a big auto parts firm. Better get that high school diploma before you even think about work . . . ."

CHAPTER 15 DRIVE FOR THE MONEY

The sun grilled the fairgrounds until the hoods of the cars were too hot to touch. Bud and Cotton took seats in the grandstand for a better view of the races. The smell of popcorn and exhaust fumes drifted along the hot breeze.

As the eight cars went out for the semi-main event, the green Maserati was directly ahead of Red. Sipping soft drinks, they listened with amusement to the fans grumbling about the Maserati. It shouldn't be allowed to race; it was too light; a freak like that destroyed the dignity of the show.

Besides, green was bad luck.

"*All* British racing cars are green," someone pointed out.

"Ship it back to England, then," someone else retorted.

"A Maserati's Italian, not English," another fan put in.

"Okay, but the driver is—"

At that moment the flag fell.

The pack leaped with a bass detonation of exhausts. The buzz-saw whine of the Maserati sliced across the deeper snarl of the American engines. The little car was slow on the jump, but gunned its way through the first-lap tangle to second place. A car hit the wall on the second lap and the yellow light burned. All the cars reduced speed and held their positions while the wreckage was carried off the track. The driver, with a slight injury, limped to the ambulance.

The instant the green light went on again, Red rammed the old Braggan Special into the standoff bars at the back of the Maserati. With his superior acceleration, he held it there, pushing the Italian car around until the Maserati picked up speed on the straightaway and outran him.

A car was black-flagged with an oil leak and left the race. Another spun out, stalled, and was pushed from the track. For eight laps the remaining cars fought their duels. The yellow car which had started in front now had a half-lap lead. Unless it developed car trouble, no one was going to catch up. Far behind it the Maserati howled along in second place, with Red going crazy trying to pass. Coming out of the turns, he would bang into it viciously; they could see him jolt the car with bruising contacts. But before he could get in position to pass, the green racer would pick up speed in the stretch and outrun him.

Cotton had an uneasy feeling that Red was bound to try something rash.

The white flag was raised; they could hear all the engines rev up for the final charge. Red got on the rail behind the Maserati and seemed to hang back for an instant. The little Italian car started to swing sideways into the turn. For an instant there seemed to be a few feet of space between the car's front wheel and the rail. Red immediately charged into the opening.

Bud winced. "The jerk! There isn't enough room—"

But Red was moving up. He shoved the sprinter's nose brashly into the tiny wedge of space. A split second later, the Maserati went into a sudden, wild spin across the track. The crowd came up with a yell. At eighty miles an hour, the green sports car hit the wall flat. A metal panel flew through the air. The car bounced off backwards and slid down the track, as a wheel came loose and rolled along beside it. Again it hit the wall. They could see the driver lurch to the side, one arm thrown high; only his safety harness held him in the seat. The wrecked car wobbled across the track as the following cars roared past. It stopped near the rail and was pushed into the infield.

By the time the driver had climbed out of the cockpit, the remaining cars were going under the checkered flag.

The crowd sat down with a sigh. Cotton looked at

Bud. They were both wondering the same thing: had Red touched the Maserati at that sacred instant of setting the car for the slide? For while it was legitimate to "nerf" a car on the straightaways, to touch it in a turn was tantamount to putting a gun to a man's head. That tiny nudge was all it took to hurl the car out of control and into the crashwall.

That was why the maneuver was outlawed on every track in the country.

They climbed down the stands and hurried through the infield to where the Maserati rested by the track. Red had parked—after bagging second place—and run down to the front turn. He was wiping his face on a red bandana as he talked earnestly to the driver of the Maserati.

"He's really bleedin'," Bud commented sarcastically.

"Think he touched him?" Cotton asked.

"What do you think? *Something* threw that car out of control—"

The driver of the sports car was sitting on one of his rear tires with his head bowed, while Red talked to him.

"—See, I hit this chunk of dirt—it must have been the size of a piston—and it set me over just enough that I—I guess we touched."

"Just enough," the other man agreed, glancing up.

The lacquered perfection of the Maserati had been ruined by a caved-in rear end and a missing wheel. Gazing at the car, Red scratched the sweaty stubble of his red hair. He was flushed with heat and sunburn;

but if you knew him, as Cotton did, you could read a tremendous satisfaction in his face at having carried off second-place money the first time out. He reached into the cockpit and moved the steering wheel to see whether the front suspension was affected.

"I guess we made contact, all right," he said, "but it sure wasn't deliberate."

"Would you swear that on a Bible?" asked the sports car driver, with a sardonic grin. He was young, not much older than Red.

Red's smile faded. "What's the matter? Don't you believe me?"

"Sure, I believe you. If I thought you'd knocked me into the wall on purpose, I'd bend a steering column over your head. They tell me you're a new driver, Red. I suppose it was just my bad luck to get too close to somebody who wasn't used to watching for clods."

Color suffused Red's already heated face. But all he said was, "I guess your car's kind of light for the sprints, anyway, fella."

The man nodded. "I'm planning to rent a U-Drive truck next time I drive against you."

". . . Punk," Red muttered, as he walked off with Cotton and Bud. Neither boy commented, and Red asked plaintively: "You don't think I knocked him off the track on purpose, do you?"

"If you didn't," Cotton replied, "you took a big chance of doing it accidentally when you tried to pass. There wasn't room for a motorcycle."

Red snorted. "Sour grapes. When you're driving, you can't get out and measure your clearance with a tape."

They said nothing. He stared at them. Then he turned sullenly and walked back through the pits, swinging his helmet by its strap.

"Poor Red," said Cotton. "All he wants is to steal the safe and get a medal for it."

They stayed at the track while Johnny Partmann, in Mako's new speedster, placed third in the trophy dash. This was the four-lap event for the four fastest cars. An hour later, Partmann won the main event. Watching Mako's face, with its dark and sourish lines, Cotton had the feeling that the Old Pro was almost sorry Partmann hadn't lost. He didn't like drivers who arrived late at the track; he didn't like cool-headed chauffeurs like Partmann and Bud; he didn't enjoy watching other people win while he sat in the pits trying to find and oil the squeak in his mechanical hand.

Now, in late afternoon, the stands were emptying. Cars were being trailed from the infield as a hot wind blew popcorn bags and programs along the scarred adobe surface of the track. A mood of loneliness and indecision settled on Cotton. The exhilaration he had felt in setting out on his great adventure had dwindled to a dreary stub like that of a burned-out Roman candle. Bud and Herb, the only two people he had felt he could really count on, had turned their backs on him.

He did not know what to say to Bud when they reached the parking lot. Their cars were parked side by side, gleaming red, lustrous yellow.

"How soon you leaving?" Cotton asked.

"Pretty soon. I've got to wait for Mr. Cunningham. He rode over with me. How about you?"

"I'll take off, I guess. Get a hamburger on the way."

Bud did not suggest joining him for a hamburger somewhere.

Cotton started the engine. He grinned and raised his arm. "Cheers," he said. He had heard it in a movie. It meant good-bye or something.

As he drove away, he gunned the engine and streaked from the lot with a shriek of skidding rubber. Just like a kid with his first fifteen-year-old car. Just exactly. His ears burned as he drove down the highway. He wished he could back up and start out all over again.

CHAPTER 16 NUTS AND BOLTS HIGH

At Yuma, in the blackness of the desert night, he crossed the Colorado River on a long bridge, and a little while later stopped at a shedlike agricultural inspection station on the California side of the state line. An officer looked at him and glanced into the back seat.

"Any agricultural products? Citrus fruits?"

"No, sir."

The officer waved him on. As he drove from the long station with its bright lights, he saw a police car parked by a building with an officer behind the wheel. It seemed to Cotton that the officer immediately sat up straight and peered after him. His heart squeezed with cold panic.

It's your own car, he told himself. How can you steal your own car?

A few minutes later he saw headlights behind him, and he speeded up a little. Seventy, seventy-five, eighty. Then he slowed down. He could outrun a police car, but not a police radio. Maybe one of my taillights is out, he thought. Maybe he wants to see my driver's license.

The officer did.

That was the first thing he asked for after he flagged Cotton to the side of the road and shone a flashlight in his face. He looked at the driver's license, glanced on the back of it for listed infractions, and handed it back.

"Out," he said.

"Huh?"

"Get out," the policeman repeated.

Cotton's insides quivered and he got out. "Lean over the hood," the officer said, motioning with his flashlight.

Cotton laid his arms on the hood and leaned across the fender, while the patrolman ran his hands over him looking for weapons.

"Raise the hood," he said, next, and Cotton loosened the hood clamps and raised it.

The engine was so clean that the officer did not have to wipe grease from it to read the engine number. He straightened with a sour smile.

"I'll give you punks credit," he said. "You're efficient. You've already sold the engine and stolen a new one for your stolen chassis."

"No, sir. I can explain that. This friend of mine . . . ."

While he told about his friend—and the two cars—and Guarantee—and all the other confusing details, the officer made notes. Cotton was sitting behind a grille in the back seat of the police car by now. There were no inside door handles, and it was a great deal like the arrangement people had who lugged large dogs around with them. Some cars stopped and people squinted in at him, but the officer motioned them on. Then a car stopped which did not move on. It was the yellow roadster, and a core of coldness melted inside Cotton and he felt like bawling.

. . . Mr. Cunningham talked to the officer and showed him some cards in his wallet. They appeared to be business cards, and the policeman took one of them and smiled.

"Is Caffery still on Juvenile?" he said.

"Yes, and one of the best men they have. I work with him regularly. We get a certain number of parolees at the school, though it's actually a vocational school."

The officer took one of his own cards from his wallet and handed it to Mr. Cunningham. "Give this to Caffery," he said. "I'll keep this card and send it back to him with a note. Okay?"

"Fine," Mr. Cunningham said. "I'll accept full responsibility for the boy."

The patrolman let Cotton out, made a call on his radio, and drove on.

The desert, big and black and soundless, rolled over them. "I'll ride with Cotton a ways," the shop teacher said.

They started on. Cotton held the speed to fifty. He

wanted to say he was grateful, but he was afraid of breaking down and getting tearful and incoherent. He just drove.

"You understand, don't you," Mr. Cunningham said, as he tried to make his long legs fit the compartment, "that you'd be in Juvenile Hall tonight if I hadn't come along? And that you may still be jailed if the used car lot refuses to waive charges against you?"

"Yes, sir."

"Bud's told me all about you. That's why I came over to Phoenix, if you want the truth. I hate to see a boy get started wrong. Now, maybe you're just a headstrong kid, or maybe you're full of some grand purpose. Nobody but you knows—and I doubt very much whether even you do. The law makes no distinction between illegal crusades and ordinary delinquency, and if you keep on like this you'll ace yourself right out of everything you really want. Do you read me?"

"Yes, sir." This man knew kids; there was no question of it. Mr. Cunningham could read him like a road sign, and you would no sooner try to bluff him than you would take a swing at a concrete wall.

"All right. Maybe your father is a hard man. I don't know, but I doubt whether he's any harder than the average. So don't try to kid me that he's Simon Legree's younger brother. I don't know why I drive all this distance just to make trouble for myself, but Bud Smith thinks you've got unusual talent in the automobile line, and he tells me there's nothing seriously wrong with you that a little effort on your part won't remedy. —Any comments?"

"No, sir!"

"All right. Tomorrow I'll make some telephone calls. If I can straighten this out, I will. If I can't—well, I'll probably see you at Newton Boldridge High when you get out of forestry camp. A lot of people take car theft pretty seriously, you know. We have some good vocational courses at Nuts and Bolts High, as the kids call it, but I'm not sure you'd be happy with the curriculum in general. As I understand it, you're aiming for a career in automotive work. Right?"

Cotton nodded.

"Fine. If I hadn't been more interested in kids than I am in cars, I'd have wound up as an engineer of some kind myself. Each to his own. That man you met today, from Detroit, probably makes fifteen thousand dollars a year designing and redesigning automobiles. Does that sound like a worthy goal for a boy like you?"

"Sure does," Cotton murmured.

"He has college degrees, of course. And native ability —the one you can't fake. If you've got it, then it will carry you through a lot of nonsense about calculus and trig that you think you'll never survive. If you haven't got it, you can't fake it. But give yourself a chance. Get your high school diploma. Give college the old college try."

Cotton nodded. Mr. Cunningham looked back through the rear window. "Pull over," he said.

Cotton pulled onto a siding in the winding foothills road above the desert. As he stopped the car, the big man beside him scrutinized him a moment, then smiled.

"I haven't been wrong about a boy in a long time,"

he said. "Don't make me sorry I went to Phoenix. If I pull it off tomorrow, the next voice you hear will probably be that of Herb Jacobs. He's a fine man—salt of the earth. If Herb had finished college, the chances are he'd be touring the speedways of the country for some big motor car company the way the chap you met is doing . . . ."

"What's Herb—" Cotton started to ask; but Mr. Cunningham was already opening the door. He worked his long frame out of the cramped front seat, waved, and walked back to Bud's car.

Cotton sat behind the wheel, dazed, for a moment. He felt as though he wanted to take notes, quickly, before he forgot everything the man had said. Calculus, forestry camp, Herb—

But right now, the main thing was to get home without being stopped again. He stuck his arm out the window, waved, and drove back onto the highway.

CHAPTER 17 THE SHED

Cotton drove all the rest of the way home from Phoenix without stopping except once for gasoline. Every police car he passed shot his blood pressure up into the top of his head, and there seemed to be a police car for every passenger car tonight.

Having reached La Costa in the small hours of the morning, he was undecided whether to leave the car at the used car lot, or to drive it home. He drove home, finally, and left it in the garage.

A light was burning in the living room. He let himself in and looked around. No one was up. He went into the family room and switched on the light. The big, beamed room was empty also. A violent hunger seized him when he looked at the refrigerator. He looked into it and found a half-consumed pie. He ate all the pie, drank a quart of milk, and found a box of gingersnaps in the cupboard. He ate a dozen, a bite to each.

Then he went to bed, throbbing with weariness. He read a racing magazine for a few minutes, until his vision began to blur, then dropped it on the floor, and turned off the light.

A moment later, the door opened. "Cotton?" his mother said. He could barely discern her in the doorway.

"Uh-huh," he said.

"Why didn't you come to tell me good night?"

"Oh, uh—I thought you were probably asleep."

"I haven't been asleep since Friday night, when the used car lot called us."

"I'm sorry, Mom. I just felt I had to get out of town for a couple of days—"

She was silent for a moment. She crossed the room and leaned over him. When she kissed his forehead, he could hear her breathing, uneven and quick.

"What's Dad going to do?" he whispered.

"What's *Dad* going to do?" she blurted. "What are the *police* going to do!"

"I met a man named Cunningham—" Cotton began.

"Yes. He called us Saturday morning from Phoenix and told us he'd keep an eye on you. Herb called, too. He's coming to see Dad tonight—"

"Tonight! It's three o'clock now—"

"Today is Monday.—Well, get some sleep. My stars! Why didn't you just shoot somebody? That would be so simple. We wouldn't have the Highway Patrol to worry about, at least."

She started to leave, then turned back quickly and kissed him almost angrily, and said: "I wish I'd had daughters!"

Cotton turned over and thrust his face into the pillow. He raised his head to say, "They'd probably have been at Phoenix with a couple of greasy hot rodders."

Cotton was studying Civics that night when the door chimes rang. "I'll get it," his father said.

They had conversed in Neanderthal grunts and growls at the dinner table. Clearly, Dr. Clark was under restrictions of some kind himself. Now and then, when he had made some outrageous statement such as threatening to send Cotton to military school or confining him to quarters for three months, his wife would invoke certain oratorical powers of her own, accomplishing the feat of securing his agreement to say nothing, not one word, until whatever crisis was on had passed.

It was Herb Jacobs at the door. Cotton could hear them talking. Dr. Clark led Herb into the room; his office opened off it. Herb wore an ancient chalk-stripe suit with lapels right out of a 1940 gangster movie. Moving slowly and in apparent pain, he followed Dr. Clark to the door of his study.

"Never should have lifted that engine block by myself," he said.

Dr. Clark made a sympathetic murmur and closed the door.

Cotton could hear their voices faintly. After a few minutes his mother turned off the television set and went into the kitchen. He could hear everything they said, then, quite distinctly.

"—Just seems to me like you're trying to make an executive out of a boy with most of his talent in his hands," Herb was saying.

"I see. Well, I appreciate your interest," said the doctor, in a tone which made it clear that he did not appreciate it.

"Not that he isn't plenty bright—he's real inventive when it comes to solving mechanical problems. It seems to me, though, that maybe you're trying to 'modify' him, the way you would a car. And I don't see how you can do that."

"You don't, eh?" said Dr. Clark.

"No. Not that Cotton isn't plenty muleheaded himself, at times," he added.

"And that's the whole problem, right there!" said the doctor, with his first show of enthusiasm. "We simply can't get through to him."

"Kids can drive you nuts," Herb agreed. "Lemme ask you one thing, though, Doc: what's the Number One problem? His schoolwork?"

"I would say so."

"You wouldn't care particularly what he did with his spare time, in other words, as long as he got passing grades?"

"N-n-no—but as long as there's an internal combustion engine in the garage, he's going to be fooling with it. It's a compulsion."

I told you, Herb! Cotton thought wearily.

"Maybe he's learned his lesson," Herb persisted. "If he hasn't, then he never will learn; and in that case, you don't have anything to lose by trying a little experiment."

"What kind of experiment?"

"Letting him build a racing car."

On the sofa, Cotton sat up straight. A *racing* car! Was Herb out of his mind?

He heard Dr. Clark say in bitter amusement, "Oh, no. *Oh,* no! Do I seem as simple as that?"

"Thought you didn't care what he did, as long as he started hitting the books?"

"Well, but—a *racing* car, Herb! That's what started all the trouble."

"But this one they'd build up at my place. I've got all the equipment, and besides, he won't be tinkering all night if the car's five miles from home. Now, to buy this privilege, Cotton would promise to stay on top of his studies, make up any low grades in summer school, and start college in the fall."

The doctor sounded impatient. "But the whole thing's ridiculous. I don't know about prices on racing cars, but I do know he's got a fortune invested in that roadster of his."

"Sure," Herb replied. "And that's where the engine, the most expensive part of it, would come from. The body would be my problem. I can always pick something up. Cotton will need a part-time job to pay his way, probably. Maybe he can even work for me, tearing cars down and the like."

A silence settled.

"Excuse my asking," said Dr. Clark, "but what exactly do *you* get out of all this?"

"Well, I'll—I'll sell him and Bud some of the parts they have to buy. I'll charge them for the use of my equipment. But mostly— I guess you don't know racing people very well," he said.

"I don't know them at all."

"Well, every racing man who can scrape up a couple of hundred dollars, unless he's got a car of his own, can't wait to sink it in somebody else's sprinter. Just for the satisfaction of seeing it win—or taking part in a project that's at least as exciting as building a moon rocket. And if the car wins, he gets a share of the purses, of course. I'll get my cut of anything the boys win."

. . . For some time now Cotton had not breathed. He took a quick, nervous breath and licked his lips. He was afraid to breathe twice for fear he would fail to hear something.

"All right," his father sighed, at last. "But, great snakes, it sounds as though he's diving into worse trouble than he's been in right along! But I promised that man Cunningham I'd try to arrive at some compromise with Cotton. So if he's really ready to work, we'll try it for a couple of weeks. I called the used car lot today and told them we'd decided not to sell the car, by the way . . . ."

Cotton lay down on the sofa quickly and held the book over his face as they came out of the doctor's office and crossed the room. A racing car! He was numb.

Herb said formally, as he passed, "Good night, Cotton."

" 'Night, Herb."

"Why not drive up to my place after school tomorrow? Something I want to show you."

"You bet. Shall I call Bud and see if he can come?"

"I'll call him."

After letting Herb out, Dr. Clark started back to his study. Halfway there, he stopped, reflected a moment, and walked over to the sofa. Cotton looked up at him. Suddenly his father smiled, reached down, and gave his shoulder a squeeze. Then he went into the study.

Cotton's mouth trembled. It was a contract, he knew. No lawyer could have put together anything more binding.

Before leaving the next day, Cotton called Bud's home, but Bud had already started for school. So he could not get any advance information there.

At three-twenty that afternoon, he turned off the county road and started up the hill just as he saw Bud's yellow roadster coming up the road behind him. Cotton led the way up the winding road to the hilltop yard. Herb was dismantling a World War II weapons carrier when they stopped beside the streetcar and jumped out. He wiped his hands, looked at them, and did one of his deep knee bends.

"Warm, ain't it?" he said.

"Yeah. What's new?" Cotton asked eagerly.

Herb plodded to a rusty soft-drink cooler beside the

steps of the car and lifted out three bottles. He uncapped them and gave each boy a bottle. Cotton took a swallow of the drink.

"What's up, Herb?" he asked. "You told us to come by—remember?"

Herb led them down a rambling aisle of automotive relics to The Shed—the mysterious structure in which he kept records or something. Cotton's scalp began to prickle. He glanced at Bud as Herb groped for a key.

"I didn't say what *kind* of racer, remember," Herb warned.

Cotton's shoulder sagged. "It's not a midget, is it?"

"No, no. Full size. Only—oh, well."

He unlocked the door. Cotton saw a flash of forest green. *Green*! The hoodoo color. Herb closed the door again, rubbing his cheek and looking guilty. "I guess maybe I should explain something—"

"Whatcha got in The Shed, Herb? *Please*!"

"It's a chassis I picked up at a race four-five years ago. It got smashed up a little—well, it was practic'ly totaled, you see. The owner kept the engine and sold me the body cheap. Always thought I'd—"

Cotton pushed him away and opened the door. The shack exhaled a breath of grease and damp earth. Bud crowded up to look over his shoulder. The afternoon sun shone on the richly lacquered skin of a racing car. The car resembled a green beetle with wheels. The forepart was extremely low, a flattened tube. The rear portion, behind the roll bar, was high, indicating a rear engine compartment. But the car was a total wreck, its front wheels twisted, the glossy snoutlike front portion smashed almost flat.

"What is it?" Cotton asked blankly.

"Cooper," Herb said.

"*Cooper*! That's a sports car."

"Right. There's a lot of fun in sports car racing, boys. I thought we'd modify it and race it at Riverside and some of the other sports car tracks around here."

"I've never driven a sports car," Bud said.

"You'll catch on. Now, that front end is ruined. But rather than look for a used front end, maybe we could get your friend, R. C. Cunningham, to build us a replica."

Bud rubbed his ear. "Gosh, I don't know— It's a different kind of racing, Herb. Sort of like riding to hounds, isn't it?"

"Sure, it's different. But if a guy can't adapt to changing times, he's going to become extinct, ain't he?" Herb chuckled.

Bud glanced at Cotton. "What do you think?"

Cotton slipped into the shed and ran his palm over a crumpled metal panel. He let himself down into the cockpit. It was cramped, but everything was finished like a gold watch, and the design was clean and functional. Like all of its kind, the Cooper was more torpedo than car. As he sat there, he tried to picture it on a dirt track. It would hug the ground as though it had suction cups, would corner and brake better than any conventional racing car that ever rolled. His pulse began to bounce.

"Why not modify it for the sprints?" he blurted.

Herb grimaced. "Oh, come on. It's too light for all that banging around."

"We could install heavy standoff bars and reinforce the frame."

"You're crazy!" Herb said, shaking his head.

Climbing out of the little car, Cotton said: "So are you, then. I never even thought of it till I heard you arguing with Mako in the restaurant."

"Heck, I was just trying to get Gil's goat! In the first place, you'd have to have a big engine, and where would you put it?"

Cotton considered the sleek metal cockscomb behind the roll bar. "It would take our Chevy engine, if we dropped the mounts . . . ."

Bud climbed into the car. He rubbed dust from the battery of instruments, turned the wheel, and tried the pedals. "Feels good," he said. "As far as sports car racing goes, though, it'd be like starting over. Don't see much point in risking my neck for a medallion to sew on my sweater."

Herb lifted off the engine cover and gazed into the empty compartment. "I just can't see it," he muttered. "Eleven hundred pounds against sixteen hundred? Huh-uh. You'd have to lengthen it and widen the track to U.S.A.C. specifications, too. No dice."

"It'd be heavier by the time we got a big engine in it. And I know you could lengthen it, because I've seen it done."

"Maybe. But the real problem would be whether it got pounded to pieces. And whether a car like this will go on a dirt track, anyway. I'm sorry this is all I got to offer," he said.

Cotton laughed. "Nobody's crying but you," he said. "I'll bet my last Cadillac we could take them. We'd have twice the traction of a front engine car. And the way these bugs handle, Bud could move in and out of the traffic like a fish."

Bud's eyes began to shine. "Another thing, Herb: if we build a standard sprinter, we're up against everybody else with the same equipment. It gets to be more of a mechanics' race—who can crowd on the most horsepower. This would be a real dark horse."

Moodily, Herb nodded. "This is one dark horse that'll need all its shoes—for luck. I'll leave it up to you kids what we build. If we can pull it off, there'll be a boom in old sports cars. But if we can't, we'll give the fans some of the funniest Sunday afternoons they ever had!"

CHAPTER 18 SPEEDWAY ASSOCIATES

That week they tore the Cooper down. What had appeared difficult suddenly looked impossible. The frame was twisted, the front suspension mangled. To cram a big engine into the small compartment they would need a hydraulic shoehorn. The radiator would have to go up front, with asbestos-wrapped pipes connecting it with the block, behind the driver.

Stripped of its hide, the Cooper was about as streamlined as a hay baler. But a small blue flame had begun to burn in Herb, transforming him from a somnolent, often dispirited mechanic to a terse, fast-moving man with things to do. All these years he had been tearing things apart; now he was going to build something—something that might make history. He was almost brusque with customers who came to the yard looking for parts. He let them browse, while he worked.

But one day when Cotton arrived from school, he was sitting dejectedly on a box, frowning at the wreckage. "What's the problem?" Cotton asked.

"*Problems*, Rover Boy."

"For instance?"

"Fuel injector. We've got to have fuel injection to be in the race."

"I thought probably you could pick one up."

"Maybe there's one under that pile of emeralds in the corner," Herb said. "Guys don't swap those things around, like old pistons. This one'll take cash."

Cotton chewed his lip. "Mr. Cunningham seems to know everybody. Maybe he could get us a price."

"I doubt it. And another thing: do we offset the engine to compensate for centrifugal force on the turns? If so, how much? It's all left turns on a speedway, don't forget."

"I guess we'll have to experiment."

"Not with offset, brother! One wrong guess and we're over the crashwall. Then, what kind of brakes? And what about the front end design?"

Cotton walked around the racer, pondering. "Bud says Mr. Cunningham promised to help us build a front end, for cost. Maybe he can figure out some of these other things, too."

Herb shook his head. "Out of his line. He may know

men who can. But personally, I think the ship is about to sink."

"Can I use your phone for an S.O.S.?"

"Help yourself."

When Cotton came back from telephoning, Herb was rigging a hydraulic jack onto the frame.

"It's all set," Cotton told him. "Mr. Cunningham will meet us in the high school shop tomorrow, after his night school class. He said he'd try to have a couple of other men there to advise us."

Herb smiled. "Crazy!" he said.

Newton Boldridge High School was twice the size of La Costa. The parking lot was still half full when they arrived. People were drifting from the lighted buildings, most of them adults with books under their arms. In the big machine shop, Bud was helping Mr. Cunningham cover some machinery. The burly, square-shouldered man took them into his office and poured coffee from a percolator on a filing cabinet.

"Bud, get the doughnuts out of the safe," he said. "The other men will be here in a few minutes."

He was full of talk and energy, enveloping them in his warmth, bustle, and good nature. Discussing the possibilities of the car they wanted to build, he made it sound quite feasible. Their enthusiasm rose. Presently the other men arrived, and Mr. Cunningham introduced them. They all sat down at a long Masonite-topped table, with scratch pads and pencils before them. One of the men was an English expatriate named Bill Wynn, a man of about fifty years who looked like a matinee idol of yesteryear. He had silver-gray hair and blue eyes in a tanned face. But he was the owner of three foreign car agencies, and his shops did most of the work for the sports car racing crowd.

Novak, the other man, was small, outspoken, and intense. His handshake left Cotton's hand aching. Novak owned a chain of auto supply shops.

Mr. Cunningham got down to business quickly. "Cotton, suppose you explain what you boys are trying to build."

Cotton's voice trembled, at first, as he tried to explain their problems and aspirations in rebuilding the Cooper. Novak rested his elbows on the table and placed his chin in his palm. He immediately closed his eyes and seemed to go to sleep. Bill Wynn made notes.

"—You want to explain the offset problem, Herb?" Cotton said finally, moving the burden to Herb's shoulders.

Haltingly, Herb explained. "I know there's a formula you can use, but I don't have it, or the math to use it if I did."

Wynn opened a large loose-leaf notebook and searched through it until he found a mechanic's guide sheet for the Cooper. He asked questions about the weight of the engine and the kind of fuel they planned to use. Then he went through some intricate mathematical maneuvers with a slide rule.

After the last *equals* sign he wrote the figure: "4½″."

"Offset it four and one-half inches to the left," he said. "That will give you 54 per cent of your weight left, 46 per cent right, for left cornering."

Cotton blinked, and Mr. Cunningham chuckled at his surprise. "It's simple," he said. "All you need is an engineering degree and a little genius. The next question concerns a fuel injector—"

But that question was lost in other matters, and Cotton feared they were never coming back to it. At last Novak roused from his torpor to gaze at them almost suspiciously.

"Do you really believe this brute will run?"

"Sure, it'll run—we hope," Herb said. "I admit it sounds a little silly—"

"It does sound silly," Novak agreed. "Personally, I think you're doomed. But if you *should* start winning races, it would be a shame if I didn't have my name on the side of your car when they take its picture for the speed magazines. Will a fuel injector for cost less fifty dollars buy me advertising space?"

Cotton looked at Bud; then both turned to Herb. Dazed with pleasure, they all nodded.

"I'll take a chance, too," Mr. Wynn said. "You can't run a car like this with ordinary brakes. How about a set of good brakes in return for my emblem on the hood?"

Cotton grinned. "The way this is going, we'll have to tow a billboard."

"And by the way," Mr. Cunningham said, "you want to save some space for your team name. Have you chosen one?"

It was Herb who replied, although there had been no discussion of a name. He tried to put on an offhand manner, but Cotton suspected that he had given the matter serious consideration.

"How about 'Speedway Associates'?" Herb offered, as if he had ideas like that all the time.

Bud winked at Cotton. "That's a winner, Herb! Sounds like two millionaire sportsmen and an Indianapolis champion."

Herb grinned sheepishly. "Instead of two wet-behind-the-ears students and an old junker!"

A week later they went to work.

The first step was to tear the engine out of the red roadster and rebuild it for the new fuel system. As long as they were taking the roadster apart anyway, they took Cotton's original engine out of Bud's yellow car and put it back in the red car, where it had come from. Herb had a good Chevy block and they put this in the yellow car, along with enough other goodies to provide Bud with a power plant that did not sound like a hot rodder's first rebuild job.

Then Cotton began rebuilding the big engine. The critical step was to lower the compression so that the cylinder heads would not be blown through the hood by the injectors. The work was exciting, but frustrating. For at five-thirty every afternoon, just as he was well started, Herb would chase him out.

"Go hit the books, Rover Boy," he would say.

Cotton would go home, wash up, and faithfully attack his homework. While it was not fun, exactly, he began to find his studies less onerous when he kept up with them.

For a while now, Herb had seemed merely to tinker.

Suddenly he had his own work to keep up, or attempt to, and the racer came second. Cotton saw that he did not really know where to start. What they needed was a rubber chassis which could be pulled fore-and-after a foot or so, then stretched crosswise to widen the wheel span.

Even after Herb was actively working on the car, they seemed to lose ground. He was always cutting a frame member with the torch, until the car consisted of dozens of small parts, like a kit. They were in Easter vacation before he finally began reassembling it. The engine itself was long since reassembled.

Most of Cotton's time now was spent lying under wrecked automobiles. Herb was always bidding on cars "totaled" in highway crashes. He would haul them home as proudly as a family cat bringing in a rabbit—sometimes an almost new car he had bought for three hundred dollars; occasionally an ancient automobile which he would handle solemnly and carefully, as though it were something particularly precious. For the older cars, for which parts were no longer manufactured, were the most valuable to a junker.

When Cotton was not busy tearing down a car and cleaning parts, he tried to bring some order to the battlefield of greasy junk within the walls of Herb's wrecking yard. He built some bins and racks to hold parts. He painted a diagram in colors and posted it near the entrance. *Headlights* were shown in one color, *Bumpers* in another, *Radius rods* in still another, and so on. Then he painted the bins corresponding colors to make it easy for parts-hunters to find what they wanted.

Herb paid him almost a living wage for his work. Cotton saved every nickel he could. If they ever got this car running, it would be as costly to maintain as a spoiled girl friend.

One day, two weeks after the new school quarter began, things suddenly began to move fast. The Cooper's exploded parts reassembled themselves as if by magnetism.

The sturdy tubular frame was complete. The new front end had been assembled on it. Into the Vee that Herb had made in a transverse chassis tube, they lowered the engine with a chain hoist. Cotton took a week linking up the cooling system with the engine at the rear of the car. Bud brought the metal panels back from the body shop where he worked. He had pounded them out and refinished them. They had picked orange and white as their team colors, and when he tore off the protective paper coverings Cotton could not believe the panels were anything but the finest china. Bud had sprayed, rubbed, and again sprayed so many coats of paint onto the metal that its surface was like a pane of glass. The rich tangerine hood and cowling were trimmed with bone-white. The chromed ram tubes of the fuel injector looked like polished silver.

One Friday afternoon Bud took off time from work to bolt the panels together. Quite suddenly, in an hour or two, the long job of rebuilding ended.

The little car rested on the ground before them like the finest model that was ever built. Awed, they realized nothing remained but to pour fuel into the tank. In silence, they stood gazing at it. Against the grease-blackened earth, surrounded by drifts of junk, the Cooper had a clean other-worldly glow. Yet no one cheered; no one seemed ready to celebrate.

Cotton himself felt sick. The car was too light, too fragile, to survive two laps of dirt-track mayhem. Its slender axles and tie rods, reaching from shell to wheels, gave it the delicate profile of a water spider. It was all slender body and wispy legs.

Herb was right: you couldn't make a bulldozer out of a bicycle.

But, hopefully, he squinted at the heavy standoff bars, reminding himself that nothing but hydraulic pressure could bend them. And the tubular frame was just as strong. The car had those strong points working for it —and not much else.

"Whattayou think, boys?" Herb asked, finally. He tried to sound hearty, but did not quite carry it off.

"Smooth," Bud said. "Miss Universe would look like a dog, compared to her."

"Is it gonna be heavy enough?" Cotton asked.

Herb stuffed in his shirt tail and reset his cap. "Never know till we try," he boomed. "How about Sunday at San Luis?"

"Okay by me," Bud said.

"I think I can get a twelve-hour pass from my C.O.," Cotton said.

And they walked around looking at it, thinking of all the money and work compressed into that orange shell, and of how a single contact with the crashwall would reduce it to scrap.

CHAPTER 19 THE CHOPPER

Early Saturday morning, they unloaded the racer at San Luis Speedway. On the basis of improved quarterly grades Cotton had wangled a dispensation from his father to stay overnight at the track. A few workmen were puttering about, watering the palms in the infield and sweeping trash from the bleachers. As soon as the engine was revving, filling the bowl with its high screech, Al Stubbings and his pit steward came hustling from the trailer office. The lanky promoter put his fists on his hips and stared at the ground-hugging orange torpedo in which Bud sat behind the wheel, his helmet coming barely above the cowling.

"Holy tomato!" he said. "What is it?"

"Sprint car," Cotton said.

Bud treadled the accelerator and the engine bellowed a wild up-and-down howl. Stubbings made an angry gesture and Bud cut the engine, beaming.

"Sprint car, my eye! It's a sports car," Stubbings rapped. "We don't run them here. Take it out of my sight."

"What's the matter?" Bud retorted. "Afraid we'll leave your Alice-blue bucket in the clods?"

"We're an outlaw track," Mel Franks declared, "but we go by Yusac specs. That thing's too small."

"Get the tape," Cotton said confidently. Everything on the car was strictly according to U.S.A.C. requirements.

Franks checked the wheelbase and track width. Muttering, he stuffed the tape measure in his pocket. "It's too light. It'll break up."

"Let us worry about that. It's going to be up front all by itself anyway."

"*That* I've got to see!" Stubbings kicked a tire, contemptuously. He could not keep them from racing, but he could make it hard for them. With his lips set, he shook his head. "No practicing here," he said. "You ought to know that. You'll have to wait till tomorrow."

In a way they felt better, since Stubbings seemed to view the little car as a threat. His attitude indicated more confidence in the car than Speedway Associates had been able to generate.

For the rest of the day Cotton and Bud tinkered with the car, running the engine hard, then checking the ignition and fuel system. It would be a miracle if they got through their first race without a major breakdown; nevertheless they wouldn't strike out for lack of effort. About four o'clock they covered the car with a tarpaulin, locked the tools and supplies in the trunks of their roadsters, and left the track.

A two-lane road carried them west to a campground at the beach. It was too early in the season for the beach crowds, and there were few campers. They pulled on trunks and body-surfed until the sun went down. Shivering, they ran back to the cars and built a fire. They heated a can of stew, then talked until the fire went out and they crawled into their sleeping bags for warmth.

In the morning they ate at a restaurant and headed back to the track. It was only nine o'clock when they drove through the gate. A few cars were already on the track, taking practice laps, and the infield looked like a gypsy camp where every gypsy owned a sprint car. They found a spot and got to work.

Their biggest job, they soon learned, consisted of explaining to people what the car was supposed to be. A few ignorant youngsters appeared impressed by the car's flashy perfection, but most of the racing crowd, who knew that a good paint job would not turn a car's wheels, smiled and had the same Stone Age jokes to make.

They warmed the engine and gears, and Bud got in. He moved around, getting comfortable. Cotton motioned to one of the pickup trucks, and the driver eased up behind the car and pushed it from the pits. Reaching the track, Bud locked the brakes while the truck pushed him, released them suddenly and the car leaped away.

Cotton went to one knee beside the track and tried to keep calm, though he was trembling. The engine sounded as rich and beautiful as organ music. But that proved nothing. A driver might test-drive a new car, and look like the winner and new champion. But he would shake his head as he got out.

"It doesn't feel right," he would say.

And it never would: the X-factor was absent. Some almost metaphysical quality which pulled everything together simply had not been built into the machine.

Cotton watched the little orange shell blaze around the oval with a roar out of all proportion to its size. After a few laps Bud drove from the track and hit the kill-switch.

"How about it?" Cotton asked.

"It's got the power, all right," Bud said. "I've got to learn to hang onto it."

Cotton sensed that he was holding something back. "What's the matter?"

Bud frowned. "All the traction's in the rear. The steering's too light."

"Then we'll change the wedge."

"It'll take more than that. We may have to make a basic change in the frame."

"Do you still want to try to qualify?"

"Sure. That's what we came for. I'll just hold the speed down a little."

Shortly before the qualifying, Mako showed up with Red. Both of them were laughing.

"My goodness," Mako said, "this must be England's

answer to the speed problem. What time do you serve tea and crumpets?"

"Right after we win the trophy dash," Bud said.

"It's some kind of car, isn't it?"

"Chevy engine, Cooper body."

Red laughed. He was dangling his gold crash hat by the chin strap, and wore a black racing shirt with white seams. "Ken Miles built a Porsche-Cooper once. They called it 'The Pooper.' "

Cotton had an inspiration. "We call this one 'The Chopper,' " he retorted.

Cotton changed the spring wedge, but from the way Bud drove his qualifying lap he knew the steering was still wrong. He came back, and they tried to make some small changes before the semi-event. It seemed that everyone who could afford a pit pass had come here today to crowd around and ask questions. Even Charlie Grimes, solemn and curious, studied the automobile and asked some questions that made them uneasy, they seemed so pointed. Some of the questions were answered in the race, when Bud started driving . . . .

The event had barely started when he began to fall behind. He seemed to have plenty of power, and on the straightaways he succeeded in passing a couple of cars. But in the turns he slowed down and they passed him easily.

The Chopper finished out of the money: sixth in a field of eight. The racing crowd, however, gave Bud a nice hand for effort.

In the windy dusk, they loaded the car on the trailer and headed home.

That night Herb poured coffee for them in the streetcar, and listened to their sad tale. "Rear engine problems," he sighed. "You'd better talk to the professors again."

The next day Cotton called Mr. Cunningham, who passed the problem along to Mr. Wynn. The auto agency man conferred with some experts in his shop. A week later, the answer came to the wrecking yard in the form of a sketch in a big envelope. Cotton examined the sketch; his stomach turned over.

According to the experts, the fuel tanks must be moved forward, heavier front standoff bars installed, and some drastic corrections made in the rear suspension. A roll cage was suggested for additional weight forward.

Herb was working twelve hours a day now, rebuilding a couple of cars for quick money after sinking so much time in The Chopper. Thus the rebuilding landed on Cotton's back.

It was early May, now, and the last rain this country would see for six months was behind. The ground was dry and warm as Cotton lay beneath the car removing bolts for the big change.

The job took three weeks. They hauled the car to Gardena Speedway, in Los Angeles, and went through the familiar routine of being ribbed while they worked fast trying to get the car in trim. Bud took some practice laps and said the car handled perfectly. But there was a crease of perplexity on his face as he got out.

"Any kicks?" Cotton asked, anxiously.

"We've lost a little acceleration. I guess we've hung on so much weight that we've lost some of the advantage of the small car. But it still squirms through the corners like an eel. Maybe we'll make it up there."

He drove a hot qualifying lap to make the main event. Charged with excitement, they worked over the car until race time. Bud crossed his fingers and climbed into the cockpit.

Red was driving in the same heat. When the race started, he gunned away from the car beside him with a visible surge of power. But The Chopper dropped back. Cotton groaned, knowing Bud was right: the take-off just wasn't there. Coming down the back straightaway, however, the orange car caught up with the leaders.

All through the twenty-lap race, that was the pattern; he lost ground coming out of the turns, picked it up on the straightaways. The problem was that they had greater developed horsepower than the other cars, less acceleration at slow speeds.

Somehow Bud brought the little car in third. They went home knowing a fifty-dollar check would be coming through the mail.

When they trailed the speedster into the wrecking yard, Herb came out on the gallop.

"How'd she go?"

They told him. He frowned and rubbed some mud from the paint. "Same old story. Jump one hurdle, stub your toe on another. Be that way, I guess, till they repeal the laws of physics."

"How about a little more compression?" Cotton suggested. He was tired, and his ears still hummed with the giant howl of the big engines.

"Risky. Might blow up. But let's try it. Then take it over to Westmoreland next week, if you can get your dad to okay the trip. It'll be the last race of the winter season over there—probably a hundred and nine in the desert already. It's a bigger track, you know, and we might have a little edge over the Offies."

Cotton had the cylinder heads milled down and got the car back in tune by Friday night. The clean, hot sound of it echoed back from the wrecking yard fences.

"She's hot enough now, boy," Herb said. "Wish I could go along with you."

"Why can't you?"

"I've got an order for a dozen 1956 Pontiac brake drums. I know I've got them, if I can just locate them. Wonder if they're still under that old Mack truck—?"

"The one with the solid rubber tires?" Cotton asked.

"You're pulling my leg," Herb said. "But, as a matter of fact, *all* trucks had solid tires for many years, and—would you believe it?—one of their biggest problems was blowouts!"

Saturday afternoon Cotton and Bud left for the desert, towing the racer on a trailer behind Cotton's roadster. Westmoreland lay in the irrigated green oasis of the Imperial Valley, eastward across the coastal mountains. There were long reaches of date palm groves, cotton fields, and truck crops. Though it was only late May, the blistering summer had already touched the desert. The hot air did not cool till midnight.

The fairgrounds were full long before race time.

Johnny Partmann was up north with the new Mako car, but the S-M team was represented by Red Hasty. Red took the old Braggan Special out and made it look like a young car again, as he dared the law of gravity to throw him over the wall. Then Bud went out in the Cooper and boomed into the lineups for the trophy dash as well as the feature!

"Man, this is a going car, now!" he said. "This is our day. When you hear that first car cross the line, it'll be our song it's playing."

Cotton checked everything. In all his life, he had never been so excited. For this was big-league competition. Even the cynical die-hards of the racing business, the men like Mako who claimed it wasn't a racer unless it had an Offie engine, showed them a little respect.

A truck with a padded bumper gave Bud a start, and he got in line for the trophy dash. When the green flag fell, he started his charge furiously. He seized second position, then began jarring away at Billy Michaels, the leader. He had all the acceleration he needed now, and he was using it.

In fact, he was about to pass Michaels on the fourth and final lap when the Cooper blew a cylinder head . . . .

That was the day Cotton realized there was no magic formula for building a speedster.

Once, on the way home, the thought came: Why not sell The Chopper and build a conventional sprinter? Start with somebody's old car, beef up the engine—? He rejected the idea. They had put in too much work on the car, taken too much ribbing. He would stick with it as long as anyone else in the team was willing.

Mr. Novak sold them parts at cost, and Cotton tore the engine down once more. Before he completed the overhaul, it was time to drop everything and study for finals.

CHAPTER 20 GLORY DRIVER

To no one's surprise, Cotton pulled down two *D*'s. They were better than *F*'s, at least—and he could bring them up in summer school.

Before he could draw a breath, summer school was in session, without even a long week end to rest up. But with his afternoons free from twelve-thirty on, he now had time to get ready for the summer racing season. All over California and Arizona, the big tracks were thundering at full bore. He and Bud worked out a schedule which called for a close-to-home race every Sunday during summer school, with a big race at San

Luis on July Fourth. Then, in August, they would head up the coast, hitting all the main tracks before returning for the opening of a new speedway at Riverside. There would be a large purse for this one, with many top-line drivers battling for it. It would be their chance to prove that Speedway Associates weren't merely a couple of oddballs who had lost their way to a sports car rally.

As far as the racing crowd was concerned, summer started on July Fourth. This year a lot of the best cars were at San Luis, where Al Stubbings had scratched up a thousand-dollar guarantee for a fifty-lap feature.

Herb took the day off to watch the Cooper run, and even Mr. Cunningham drove up. By noon, the air was singed with bluish hot-oil fumes, and the bowl resounded to the howling of big engines. The Chopper had never run better: Bud made the list for the fifty-lap feature and was only a half-second off the pace for the trophy dash.

Something odd happened while Herb and Cotton put the car in final tune for the race.

Billy Michaels had just won the trophy dash in his Briggs Special. He was an aggressive little driver who competed hard and made few errors. Michaels came over to where Cotton was working, carrying a paper cup of coffee, and he and Bud talked out of earshot for a while. At last he tossed the cup in a barrel and said, loud enough for Cotton to hear,

"Be thinking about it, though, huh?"

"Sure. I'll think about it," Bud said.

Be thinking about what? Cotton wondered. He was too busy to ask.

Bud came over to the car. "How about a little more weight up front?" he asked.

Cotton frowned. "Your right front wheel was already a foot off the ground!" he protested.

Bud said, "Let's go for a foot and a half, then."

Herb changed the weight, though it worried Cotton to think of all that weight on a single wheel while the car blasted through the turns.

At race time, Herb repeated his old warning: "Drive as fast as you want, but don't drive over your head."

The cars circled the track. Red had qualified seventh and was starting in the back row, since the track was using the regulation start for the holiday races.

At the flag, eight engines bellowed with their heavy artillery. Michaels took the lead in the first turn. Cotton stayed on the motorcycle jump to watch the action, his mouth dry with excitement.

On the second lap, a car skidded broadside and stalled. The following car slammed into it and flipped upside down. There was the terrible graveyard hush that followed a serious accident. But, as usual, both drivers crawled from the wreckage, muttering in disgust but unhurt. The wreckage was dragged away and Cotton saw Stubbings beaming over the excitement he had provided his customers.

When the green flag turned the cars loose again, the lineup was Michaels, Johnny Partmann, a white car with a big red 11, then Bud in fourth place. Red was right behind, banging away at the Cooper's nerfing bars. The little car held tight. Cotton winced at each impact. Every time the orange car raced, it was like watching kids play catch with his mother's crystal goblets. The conventionals looked so squat, powerful, and mean that he wondered why he had ever thought a sports car could be strengthened enough to stand them off.

Beside him, a man said, "Ever ask yourself what you're trying to prove with this car, Cotton?"

Cotton glanced at the man. It was Mr. Cunningham, carrying his coat over his arm. He was surprised to see him, and equally surprised at the question.

"That it'll move, I guess," he said. "Same thing everybody else is trying to prove."

"And that's all?"

"I don't know—that we're not as crazy as they say, I suppose."

"Revenge, you mean?" Mr. Cunningham raised his brows.

"I don't think so. Whatever I'm trying to prove, I want to prove it to myself as much as to the rest of them."

"Because that would give you confidence, wouldn't it?" Mr. Cunningham said. "Confidence to tackle the next thing."

"Maybe. Seems like every box you open in this business, there's another one inside it."

"Smaller, though. At least opening the first box makes the next one *seem* smaller. Seems to me you've already proved your point," he added. "You're competing against some of the best of them today."

A chill uneasiness blew on Cotton's skin. He felt a tension like that before a firecracker went off.

"Can you stand some bad news?" Mr. Cunningham asked.

"Bad news?"

"Bud's had an offer to join the Briggs team as an alternate driver. Briggs got Michaels to pitch it to him. He's had his eye on him for some time, apparently."

A cold weight settled on Cotton. He wondered numbly how he could have failed to see it coming.

"Drivers like Bud are pretty scarce," Mr. Cunningham said. "They stand out like Olympic athletes."

But I spotted him first! Cotton thought, angrily. After a moment he managed a shrug.

"Guess I'll have to come out of retirement and go back to driving," he said.

"I thought you didn't particularly like driving?"

"Who else is going to drive the car?"

"There are plenty of competent young drivers around who'd give their left arm to take Bud's place."

"Competent isn't good enough," Cotton said. "All the guys out there right now are *good*. With a big G. That's how they got there."

Mr. Cunningham sighed. "I know. But I've known Bud for a long time, too, and I'm sure he wouldn't walk out on you without finding you a replacement."

"How many good drivers would want to compete in The Chopper?" he said. "All the big ones are used to having their money come in regularly."

Mr. Cunningham did not answer that one. It answered itself: the successful drivers were already lined up. They might drive two or three times a week, which meant a professional crew and a lot of money behind them. You could wrap it up in one phrase, Cotton decided:

I knew him when . . . .

They watched Bud systematically hammer at the car ahead of him and wait for the breaks. A long race was made-to-order for him. When the white Number Eleven car went wide, he jammed himself into the hole and squirmed by. He was behind Partmann, now, but passing Johnny was like catching fish by hand. The wily veteran synchronized his moves with those of the man behind him, while jabbing away at the car ahead. When Bud tried to pass wide, Partmann went wide; when Bud dived for the rail, the blue car was already there plugging the hole.

Bud never fathomed the way to pass the man. He had to settle for third-place money. He was underpowered for a short track—that was his main problem. But in finishing third, he looked like a winner. He got a good round of applause when he took the checkered flag.

Cotton shoved his hands in his pockets and wandered back to meet him and get the news. Why should Bud waste his time driving a freak, when he could be out there chauffeuring a big sprinter with somebody else picking up the tab and paying him a percentage of the win money?

So now The Chopper went back in Herb's shed, to dream of the time it took third at San Luis.

They pushed the car onto the trailer. In the late afternoon, a parade of bright but grimy cars trailed through the dust to the gate. In the distance, the Fourth-of-July's-end traffic boomed along the freeway.

"Wish I knew what to do next," Herb mourned. "On a mile track we could take them all."

Cotton raised and locked the gate to hold the car

on the trailer, but he said nothing. He was still waiting. Bud had not mentioned the Briggs offer. A pickup truck with the gold Briggs emblem on the door pulled in beside them; a Briggs mechanic Cotton recognized was at the wheel. At his side, Billy Michaels thrust his head out the window.

"Gonna let Briggs put you in the driver's seat?" he called. Michaels' black hair was roached like a mule's mane. He looked like any young gas pumper from the neighborhood service station, but he was one of the ablest drivers in the country.

"On the bench, you mean?" Bud called back. "I'm driving now, sport."

Michaels waved and the truck moved on.

"I've got a chance to wax cars for Briggs this summer," Bud explained to Cotton. "The way they put it was 'alternate driver.' You know how many times I'd alternate for Billy."

"Grab it," Cotton said. "With all Briggs' money, he might add another car any time."

"I've got a car," Bud said. "And I get to drive it whenever it's running."

"Did he offer a guarantee?" Herb asked.

"Sure. But I like to drive, not warm the bench. On this team, I'm the star."

"Glory driver, huh?" Cotton said.

"Every driver's a glory driver. And right now we're so close to glory with The Chopper that I'd be a fool to quit."

"You may not get a chance like this again," Cotton told him, hoping he wouldn't believe it.

"If I look good now, I'll look even better when I start winning races. Besides," Bud said, laying his hand on the automobile, "I happen to like this crazy little bucket. I know it better than the Lone Ranger knows his horse—I helped build it, and I hear he built Silver from a kit."

They were ready to travel now, and they all piled into the front seat of Herb's old truck. Sitting between them, as they rolled down the highway, Cotton basked in a feeling of comradeship as warm as a campfire. They understood each other. Somehow that seemed as important as winning races.

CHAPTER 21 ASCOT

All through July, the racing wars blazed on a dozen fronts. But Cotton and Bud were in the lines only once a week. Even so, Cotton's undersized partner was rapidly learning his machine and putting finesse on his car handling.

With Red, it was the story of a minor-league skyrocket. Nearly every morning Cotton would open the paper and see Red's name in the race results. He was competing in races all over Southern California and Arizona, and winning a few, too. One reason for his success was that Partmann drove the big races for the big purses, while Red toured the lesser tracks in the small towns. Yet you couldn't call sprint car competition easy anywhere.

Bud was putting in extra time at the body shop to justify the time he wanted to take off after Cotton finished summer school. With a two-week vacation coming, he hoped to tack on another two weeks, giving him a full month for the Grand Tour. They would be on the road the entire month of August, working north up the state, and returning the first week in September for the opening of the new speedway at Riverside. This would be the biggest event in California's racing summer: fifty laps for a big purse.

Summer school was less of a drag than Cotton had anticipated. He liked the quiet, half-empty halls and small classes. Finally one day, after the six-week session ended, he came down the grimy cement steps for the last time, with an envelope in his hand. He sat on the bottom step, opened the envelope, and took out his report card. A *B* in Civics! A *B*-minus in English!

He was pleasantly stunned. Raising his head, he gazed across the green avocado groves. Then a great glee swept through him, and he scrambled up and ran toward the parking lot. Time to pack. In forty-eight hours, they would be heading up the coast.

"You've got too good sense to fool around with liquor and cigarettes, and all that nonsense," Cotton's mother said, with a question mark in her voice.

Cotton shook his head. "For Pete's sake, Mom! I'm eighteen now."

"That's just the point," said his father, smiling. "The dangerous age—zero to eighteen."

Cotton was packing the last of his tools and spare parts. Without slowing down in his work, he stuffed a grease rag in with his socket wrenches and closed the case. "Look on me as zero," he said. "Zero in the standings, zero to spend on nonsense."

His parents smiled, seeming embarrassed at having brought it up. "I've fixed up four casseroles for your first week," his mother said. "They're packed in dry ice. The man said it would last a long time, if you keep the cooler closed. There's that tuna and potato chip dish you like—a meat loaf—spaghetti—"

"Don't thaw anything until you're ready for it," Dr. Clark put in quickly. "Food should be kept either hot or cold, never warm. If there's trouble of any kind, call us collect. I'll wire money, or drive up."

Cotton struck his brow. "Relax! Where I'm going to be they have banks, and doctors, and everything."

Carrying two suitcases, Bud arrived in La Costa on the bus. Cotton picked him up at the drugstore from which he had called, and they headed for Herb's. The plan was to carry everything in Herb's old stake-body truck, a Dodge Power-Wagon, towing the car on the trailer. Lights were on in the streetcar, but the big lot was dark. As the headlights swept the truck and trailer, Herb came from the car. They hitched up the trailer, and Herb explained some idiosyncrasies of the truck. He suggested things to do and not to do to get more performance out of the Cooper.

At last there was nothing left to say. He offered his

hand and both of the boys reached out to grip it at once.

"Wish I could go along," he sighed. "I'll make Riverside sure, though. Any questions, call me up."

"Any advice about liquor and women? It's customary."

Herb shook his head. "Not exactly. But it might be a good idea to take along a bag of smooth round stones."

"What for?"

"Ain't that what David killed Goliath with? So go thou prepared—because on those big tracks, you two are gonna be a couple of underpowered shepherd boys if I ever saw any."

They gripped hands again, and Cotton sent the lumbering old truck down the road. They spent the night at his home, and just before daybreak drove down to the highway and headed north.

That afternoon they rented space in a rundown trailer court on the east side of Los Angeles. They tinkered with the car until dark, ate at a restaurant, and returned to spread sleeping bags in the back of the truck. Withered leaves from an old pepper tree drifted down on them all night. In the morning they drove to the track.

Ascot Speedway was a very old track in a shabby area of the city, but the noise and confusion of the place were completely modern. They drove into a rattling roar of cars warming up. A half-million dollars worth of speed equipment sparkled in the dust. Teams of professional mechanics were setting up their machines. They found a place not far from the Stubbings-Mako team. Charlie Grimes and another mechanic were working on the big blue car, while Mako lounged on a stack of doughnut-shaped tires, pointing to something at the rear of the sprinter. Johnny Partmann was talking with another driver.

"On your toes," Cotton said. "This may be the day you run in the same race with Johnny Partmann!"

"Are you kidding?" Bud retorted. "Partmann better ride that machine, or he won't be in the same race with me!"

But despite his optimism, he barely qualified twelfth in a field of fifty cars. He made the thirteen-car main event with a split-second leeway, so that he started in the sixth row, about as far behind as you could get without being in the turn. He had thirty laps in which to make his way to the front, but from the first blasting instant of the take-off, he drove as though the race was almost over. In the first ten laps, he quarterbacked himself into sixth position. But then, from the tenth to the twentieth laps, he was stuck behind another car. Two cars went out with engine trouble and a third hit the wall and had to be pushed from the track. Partmann was riding in front, a white and gold machine behind him.

Sometime after the twentieth lap Cotton realized the Cooper was beginning to move up—to fifth place, fourth—and now it was dueling for third. He watched, and finally saw what Bud was doing. Coming into the turns, he went in deeper before cutting power—deeper than the heavier car he was passing dared to. At the last instant, he braked and slid into perfect position. It was great strategy—if it did not backlash.

Chewing his nails, Cotton tried to forget the brakes. If they faded, it would happen as unexpectedly as glass breaking. Bud would be roaring into the turn at over a hundred miles an hour, with no brakes at all.

The orange car crept around the third-running car and went for second. The fans had finally noticed the little dark-horse entry stealing bases; they cheered it on. Bud caught Partmann in a turn and they came out wheel to wheel. Johnny shoved the gas pedal down and pulled ahead. Near the end of the chute Bud started to overtake him. But now it was time to cut power. Partmann realized that, if he eased up, the Cooper would pass and claim the rail. He also knew that, if he did not, his car would get away from him.

He cut power. Bud surged past. Immediately he banged the brakes on and went into a screaming power skid. Shaking, Cotton watched him slide up to the loose dirt along the crashwall. Bud wrenched away at the wheel and somehow held it in control.

Partmann, having his own troubles with a breakaway car, was powerless to capitalize on Bud's bad slide. He shot from the turn a length behind. The big Offenhauser engine emitted an angry shriek and the Special plowed after the orange miniature skimming along yards ahead of it.

The crimson figure of the starter stood at the edge of the track, checkered flag raised. The flag slashed twice—once for the Cooper, once for the Special . . . a yard behind.

Weak-kneed, Cotton sat on the ground and listened

to eight hundred dollars worth of applause booming from the grandstand.

Hurrying back to the truck, he passed Mako's crew. There were enough tools, tires, and fuel cans scattered around to outfit a country garage. The blue car had just arrived and Partmann killed the engine and climbed out. He pulled off his helmet and mask and dropped them wearily, a hawk-faced man with tension etched into the corners of his eyes. Mako uttered some angry statement which Cotton could not understand. But the driver, opening the neck of his coveralls, glanced up in surprise, and frowned.

"Isn't a second good enough for you once in a while? The kid was up today, that's all."

"A kid in a back-yard racer!" Mako said.

Partmann stared at him, tight-lipped. "If you want to talk *cars*," he said. "I told you before that the weight on this bucket is all wrong. If you want me to win all of 'em, you'll have to spend some money on it."

"Forget it," Mako's head mechanic said. "Can't win 'em all, Gil."

Mako laid his hand on Partmann's shoulder. "Tell you what, Johnny," he said, with a jeering grin. "I can't rebuild the car to suit the tenant, but I'll repaint it for you. How'd you like a nice panty-pink?"

For a moment, Cotton thought Partmann was going to swing on the old raceways bruiser. Then he slapped Mako's hand away and said:

"Why not have your mouth taped and *watch* a race

sometime, Gil? You might notice we're driving different than when you were nerfing the opposition off the tracks—"

Smack!

Mako's fist struck Partmann high on the forehead with a meaty impact. Partmann reeled back into the car, groped for a handhold, and sat on the ground. Dazed, he looked up at Mako.

"For Pete's sake, Gil!" Charlie Grimes protested.

Partmann scrambled up. He rubbed his fist into his palm; then, looking at the other's artificial hand, he shrugged and dropped his arms to his sides.

"You've got my address," he said. "Just send my check there."

Cotton walked off to tell Bud.

". . . That's the Old Pro's hard luck," Bud said. "He just lost the best driver in the Western circuit."

Cotton wrinkled his forehead and considered. "Wonder who he can get to take Johnny's place this late?"

"He's in trouble," Bud agreed. "All the top-line wheelers are already under contract."

Cotton snapped his fingers. "Red! It's got to be him."

"To drive the Special? I doubt it. He isn't ready."

"What's the difference, if Mako thinks he is? Red buys his big-mouth line all the way, and that's what Mako likes in a driver."

"I'll believe it when I see it," Bud said. "In the meantime, we just knocked over our first big prize. We're having steak tonight!"

They decided to remain overnight in the trailer court, heading for the hot Central Valley in the morning for their next race. In the morning, Cotton pulled a wheel to examine the brake lining, after the punishment of the grueling fifty-lapper. When he looked at the lining, he stared in disbelief.

"What's the matter?" Bud came over to look at it.

Between the liner ring and the drum itself was a thin, ragged crack. He squatted down and looked at it. "How much longer would it have lasted?" he asked.

"About a lap."

Cotton tapped the liner ring with a hammer and it rang with an off-key chime. He struck it twice more and it broke loose from the drum. They looked at each other, and Bud slumped onto the trailer and rubbed his neck.

"I thought I had it licked," he muttered. "If I couldn't outrun them, I'd outbrake them. I wondered why Johnny didn't try to stay with me. Guess he learned about brakes young."

Cotton tossed the liner ring aside. "You did have it licked," he said. "We're not going to put our paws in the air just because the brakes broke down."

"Funny. When I look at that thing, I lose all desire for speed."

Cotton was quiet for a while. "We'll have to go to heavy-duty brakes. Standards are Mickey Mouse stuff anyway. How many dirt-track drivers really use the brake? Practically none. But sports car chauffeurs use the brakes as much as the gas pedal."

As soon as they were packed, they drove to a sports car supply house in Hollywood and priced brakes. In the end, they had to buy new wheels as well, and even with trade-ins the cost came to three hundred dollars for the change. Without the eight hundred dollar win-money from Ascot, they would have had a big bite taken out of their bankroll, painstakingly accumulated all spring and summer. They had borrowed a little money on their street machines, sold a few parts, and Cotton had torn down all those old junkers for Herb. The sum looked big—but in this sport one wreck could wipe them out.

The new wheels had spokes that were broad and curved, like the blades of a fan; the dealer said they were the best thing he knew for racing except the even more costly disk brakes.

With new running gear installed, they set out in midafternoon for Bakersfield. Just before sunset they reached a high pass in a range of mountains. A sign pointed the way to a campground near the highway, and they decided to eat in the pine-scented coolness before winding on down the Grapevine Grade into the valley. Five minutes among the trees, with the fragrance of pines and the tinkling music of a creek, and they decided to stay through Tuesday and not venture into the valley until the afternoon of the race.

On Tuesday they worked on the car and relaxed in the clean mountain air. On Wednesday afternoon they drove down the grade into the heat haze of the Central Valley. Uneasiness brooded in the cab of the truck. Tonight would be the first time they had run under floodlights; the first time for the new brakes, too.

Nearing the speedway, they began to see other racing cars on trailers. In the line going through the gate to the track, Cotton glimpsed the S-M Special. "Who's in the truck?" he asked quickly.

Bud opened the door and stood on the running board for a better look. "Can't see—wait a minute!" he said. And he chuckled. "How about that!"

"Mako?"

"No. You were right the first time. Red!"

The blue sprinter moved through the gate and out of sight. Later, while they were getting set up in the infield, Red strolled over. Next to them, a car was raising clouds of dust as it warmed up with a deafening racket. Red was eating a hot dog, and a Coke bottle was thrust into his hip pocket. He had acquired a sunburn somewhere in his travels, and his freckled face was peeling. But nothing could peel that cocky grin from his face.

"Where you been?" Cotton asked him.

Red waved the hot dog. "Everyplace it's hot, and the purses are small. Hey, listen," he said to Bud, "I'm putting you down for an old set of piston rings for what you did for me."

"What did I do?"

"You brought me back from the boondocks. Oh, I was piling up points, and I've been getting my guarantee money right along. But Weedpatch, Arizona, is a long way from the big time. Sunday night I won twenty dollars in a thirty-lap race!"

"You're really taking Partmann's place?" asked Cotton.

"That is correct. What a phony! He's hauled freight and gone East." He took a drink from his bottle and walked around The Chopper with a thoughtful expression. "It's kind of cute, at that," he said. "Strictly a one-time winner, like Gil says, but you'll have fun with it before the novelty wears off." He dropped the bottle on the ground.

"By the way," Bud suggested, "in hot weather it's a good idea not to follow me too closely. I drink root beer as I drive, and you might run over one of my empties."

Red looked down. He kicked the bottle he had just dropped. "Thanks. I'll play safe and stay ahead of you. See you around, huh?"

Bud picked up the empty bottle Red had dropped and threw it into a trash barrel. A bottle worth a two-cent deposit could ruin a hundred-dollar tire.

"Your old buddy'll do for a punk till they invent something better," he said.

Bud qualified for the feature, along with Red. Watching Red drive, Cotton had to admit that he had taken on polish. He handled his machine well and drove more conservatively—possibly because he was getting used to the car.

By midpoint of the thirty-lap race, Bud had worked from sixth place to third. Red, his daring backed by a fast, responsive car, had moved from second position to first. He was riding easy, until suddenly he glanced back to see the Cooper outrun the number two car and grab the rail.

Cotton could hear the Special's big Offie engine hit

a higher note as Red poured in the fuel. He had a two-second edge, but the orange car was on his tail like a killer missile. Coming into the front turn, Red swung into a flat slide that brought spectators to their feet. A graveyard hush settled over the Mako team, near Cotton at the track's edge. The redhead, working hard, brought the Special back under control. Cotton saw Charlie Grimes use his cuff to wipe his brow. But Red had lost distance on the error, and the Cooper was moving in for the kill.

Cotton heard Mako's voice. "Charlie! Where are the binoculars?"

He looked around. Grimes took a small pair of field glasses from a pocket of his coveralls. Mako put them to his eyes and watched the Cooper blaze down the stretch and into the turn.

"I thought so. He's throwing oil."

The mechanic took the glasses and studied the car on the back chute. "Well, it's throwing something—"

Cotton hurried to where the two men stood and extended his hand. "Can I have a look?"

Mako shoved the glasses inside his jacket. "You jokers better start bringin' your own equipment to the track. You've got an oil leak. This is one for the starter—"

Cotton stayed with him as he headed through the spectators toward the starter's spot. "It's not oil," he argued. "If it's anything, it's a radiator leak."

"It's oil," Mako snapped, "and your beautiful assistant's all done for tonight."

The starter was standing with another official, a collection of flags at his feet. "Black-flag that orange wagon," Mako told him.

The starter turned. "Who says?"

"I say. It's throwing oil."

Putting Mako's glasses to his eyes, the official watched the car pass.

"I don't think it's oil," Cotton said hastily. "There's oil on the track, but it was the car that blew a piston in the last race that left it."

The starter lowered the glasses. "There's *something* dripping, all right . . ." he agreed.

"What are you going to do—wait till somebody piles up to black-flag him?" Mako demanded.

The official picked up a flag rolled on a long dowel, as Cotton pressed between him and Mako.

"There's only two laps left," he argued. "He's not losing much anyway! Give us a break."

"If it's gasoline, you could lose your machine and your driver. If it's oil, it may bust out in gallons."

As Bud came around again, the starter chopped the black flag down across his hood, and the little orange car began a salvo of backfiring. Bud slowed and left the track.

Cotton watched Mako take a cigarette he had worn perched over his ear and strike a match for it. As the driver took a deep lungful of smoke, grinning, Cotton suddenly plucked the cigarette from his lips and threw it to the ground.

"Sorry," he said. "You heard the man. That car might have been dumping gasoline."

He heard Mako swear as he went back to meet Bud.

CHAPTER 22 THE SYSTEM BREAKS DOWN

As the floodlights expired one by one with an orange glow, the boys left the track. They drove to a farming area north of town and made camp by a drainage ditch. The slow, heavy currents gurgled through a culvert, a relaxing sound after the hours of screeching engines and the disappointing end of the race.

While Bud set up the cots, Cotton inspected the engine. He traced the trouble to a leaky scavenger pump in the fuel injector. With a sigh, he tossed the tools aside and crawled onto his cot. A yellow moon floated in a velvet sky. He felt numb with fatigue.

"What was it?" Bud asked.

"Scavenger pump."

"That swindler! I wasn't throwing oil. Let's protest."

"Maybe he was right. The engine could have caught fire."

"It wasn't leaking that much. Did you look at the brakes?"

"I pulled the right front. The drum's okay, but the lining's shot."

"So what's the answer?"

"Harder lining, if we can find it."

"When's the Oakland race?"

"Week and two days," Cotton said. "Fifty laps. But it's a mile track, so there'll be less braking."

"But higher speeds when I do brake. Know what I think?" Bud said, disconsolately. "The system smells. *That's* the answer."

"There's an answer," Cotton insisted. "Maybe it's harder lining. We've got the Fresno race Friday night to try it out. If it doesn't work, we'll enter the truck in destruction derbies and make enough money to get home."

In five minutes they were both asleep.

They located brake lining in the big farming town of Fresno, installed it, and found a drag strip on which to try it out. Bud rated it perfect.

By race time Friday night, Bakersfield was no more than an embarrassing memory. The only race that really counted, anyway, was the next one. Midway through the main event, however, the engine blew a head gasket and the car came limping off the track.

Forlornly, they watched Red carry off second-place money. Cotton suspected that if Briggs offered Bud another chance driving for him tonight, he would never see him again before fall.

They barnstormed around Northern California for a week, marking time before the big fifty-lap race at Oakland the following Sunday, with its thousand-dollar guarantee.

On the day of the race, they reached the track early and saw the morning fog dissolve and a bright blue day take its place. It was the kind of day when even a man in a 1923 Essex might feel tempted to take a few hot laps. Bud was full of confidence. Right from the green flag, he drove hard and aggressively. Cotton had the feeling that no one could stop him today. The orange car moved up steadily until it was on the pipes of the car in first place. For ten laps it stayed there; then Bud seemed to let up a little.

A gap opened. Other drivers immediately jumped on him. Red took him on a turn and two more cars charged past. Chagrined, Cotton watched the Cooper finally head for the pits.

Bud pulled off his helmet and crawled wearily from the cockpit.

"What happened?" Cotton asked.

"Brakes. No pedal."

Cotton touched a drum: it was smoking hot. While Bud got out of his coveralls, he pulled the wheel and examined the brake.

"The lining's perfect. The brakes failed because the drums warped. As soon as they cool, they'll be as good as ever."

"Good," Bud said. "I'll go back when they cool and grab off last place."

A few minutes later they heard the loudspeakers announce that Red Hasty, of La Costa, California, had piloted his Stubbings-Mako Special to first place.

Bud brought some cold drinks from the truck and they looked at the little race-track jewel into which they had poured so much money and faith. It had everything but the ability to win races. Just a little smaller, Cotton reflected, and it would be the perfect gift for the charm collector who had everything.

". . . I was talking to a man at Sacramento last week while you were driving," Cotton said. "He liked the car. Wanted to trade his sprinter for it with a little cash thrown in."

"What's he got?"

"An old rail job—fixer-upper. We'd be racing again in a couple of weeks, I guess."

"Racing? Or just driving?"

Cotton lifted his shoulders. "That's the gamble. We haven't been exactly sensational with this crate, remember."

Bud kicked a tire so hard he winced. "I give it the best years of my life, and what do I get? Laughs."

Cotton kept still. He knew the next change he wanted to make, but he had such a gift for being wrong that he was determined to let Bud make the decision this time.

"What about disk brakes?" Bud asked, at last.

"What about them?"

"They're the best, aren't they? We've licked everything else about the car. Why sell it to some ungrateful hot rodder who wouldn't appreciate it? He'd probably put disks on it himself, and get credit for developing the New Breed."

"Couldn't have that," Cotton agreed.

"How long would it take to change over?"

"Few days—and a few hundred dollars. We've got two weeks till the Riverside race."

"No problem, then," Bud said. "We could convert and try the brakes at San Luis next week."

"*Or,*" Cotton said, "we could go on hitting thirty-lappers the rest of the summer and make some money for next summer."

"We're too big for the Little Leagues," Bud said. "I'm ashamed of you. We're going to be the first hot rodders on the moon, or my name isn't Last Place Smith. Come on—let's get packing."

CHAPTER 23 IT'S THEIR RACE TRACK

By next week end, the Cooper had new brakes and the bank account was down to a bare three figures. Racing was becoming the sport of millionaires. It was now late August, with summer running out fast and the Big One coming up next week. Even though San Luis Speedway was not exactly Indianapolis, it was their last race before Riverside, which would be the last of the summer.

And once again they were driving an untested car.

To Cotton's astonishment, his father expressed a desire to see a race, so that he might know for certain what it was he disapproved of. Cotton rounded up a pair of white pit pants for him and they drove up Sunday morning. During the qualifying, they stood by the track and Cotton tried to make everything clear.

"It's kind of hard to explain. Everybody drives the best lap he can, and his time determines what 'heat' he drives in, and what order he starts in."

The Chopper shrieked under the wire to start its timed lap. Dr. Clark made a megaphone of his hands. "That's not so complicated!" he shouted.

"Yes, but the fastest cars start at the back. Stubbings says it gives the slower cars a chance. It also gives the fans a chance to see some wrecks. The fast cars have to get by the slow ones up front, and some green drivers will try anything to keep from being passed."

"I see. The only thing I don't quite understand," said the doctor, "is why people take such risks in the first place."

Cotton nodded. "That's the one I can't explain. But maybe you'll get the feel of it, sort of, while you watch them run . . . ."

The little orange car easily qualified for the feature. It would start in the third row, behind Red. The cars opened up with a great, vibrating roar that shook the stands. Seconds later, two cars tangled in the turn. Cotton had almost forgotten what life was like at San Luis. Moments later, the survivors blasted on at the same fast place?"

Dr. Clark was fascinated by the speed and power of the cars. "It doesn't seem possible that cars could take a turn at that speed," he said. "Everything's against their staying on the track."

A blue car screamed by and skidded into the front turn. "That man drives as if he were crazy!" Cotton's father said.

"He is crazy. That's Red!"

"Well, well! He looks pretty sinister in the mask and all. Is he ahead?"

"Yes. Bud's driving third. He could be up front, if he wanted to pour it on. This is more of a test of the new brakes."

A few minutes later his father asked: "What's Red doing–jettisoning fuel to lighten his car?"

Cotton tried to catch a look at the blue car, but it was already out of view in the backstretch. "What do you mean?"

"There's something leaking out of the car."

Cotton squinted at the Special as it slid from the back turn and passed them again. Plainly, he made out a thin spray of oil beneath the car. Without a word, he turned and headed toward the starter.

". . . What oil?" Mel Franks, the pit steward, complained. Mel was standing beside the starter.

"Don't try to kid the experts, Mel!" Cotton retorted. "Red's losing oil in every turn. Look at the track."

"Get lost," said the starter, his eyes on the cars roaring by. "It's water."

Anger flashed in Cotton's head, and he picked up the black flag from the collection at the man's feet. Franks knew, and the starter knew, that Red was throwing oil. But because it was their car and their track, they intended to keep Red running long enough to win the race. He thrust the black flag at the starter.

"Do your duty," he said.

Franks yanked the flag from his hand, his pudgy features reddening. "Get out of here! We've got a race to run."

Dr. Clark had arrived in time to hear the exchange. Suddenly, to Cotton's amazement, he pulled the flag from the pit steward and pushed him out of the way. Stepping onto the track, he waited for Red to emerge from the back turn. Franks tried to recover the flag, but Cotton, who was inches taller than he, blocked him.

Coming out of the corner, Red's car sprayed a thin stream of oil onto the brick-hard surface of the track. Already the slick adobe was becoming oiled-up where he had passed. Cotton's father whipped the black flag back and forth as Red passed, but the big blue car gunned on by without cutting speed.

The starter snapped at Franks: "Get a cop, Mel. This idiot's going to get himself run over and ruin the race."

Cotton touched his father's shoulder. "It's their track, Dad. We can protest later, but I'm taking Bud out before anything happens."

His father angrily shook his head and let him take the flag. Then, from the south turn, there was a screech of rubber. The starter threw a glance down the track, seized his yellow caution flag, and stepped onto the track. Cotton peered toward the turn and caught his breath. In starting his slide, Red had let his car get away from him. A dark smear of oil showed where his tires had failed to bite and had thrown the car into a spin.

Red was fighting the wheel as the car skidded rear-end-first into the crashwall. The car hit hard with a jangle of metal and bounced off. On the raised bank, spectators scattered. The car whipped around and Red could be seen frantically reversing his wheel. A few lengths behind, Bud tried to brake and began to fishtail as he hit the slick. The Chopper smashed the blue car in the front end; then another car collided with Bud. As the Special skidded around, Red's arms flew high—a bad sign. Only an unconscious driver released the wheel. Red smashed into the wall again with an unnerving thudding and clanking. A wheel flew into the air. Cars were clashing around in a bright pinwheel of ruination. Suddenly the blue car performed an unbelievable flip and fell back upside-down.

Cotton shuddered. There was a hush. Then the yellow lights went on and men began running onto the track with fire extinguishers.

The ambulance attendant was a young man in a white shirt and pants. He kept saying, "He's okay. He's okay." They had carried Red to the edge of the track and placed him on a litter behind the ambulance. Special policemen were trying to prevent the curious from stepping on the injured boy. Blood soaked one leg of his coveralls. His face was white. Dr. Clark, who had got his bag from the car, knelt beside Red. He ran down the long zipper of Red's coveralls and used a sharp knife to slit the pants leg. Blood welled thick and dark from a cut in the boy's thigh.

Bud stood with Cotton beside the ambulance. Except for a bruised shoulder, Bud was all right. Cotton turned away. "Let's go over to the truck," he said.

. . . It seemed a long time ago that he and Red had built a dragster together. He was thinking of Red as he was then. He and Bud sat on the trailer and waited. After a while the ambulance pulled onto the track and rolled toward the gate.

The announcer said, "He's gonna be okay, folks! He's wavin' to show you he's all right. See?"

As the ambulance passed, Cotton could see the attendant moving Red's arm back and forth in a semblance of a wave. His father sat beside the boy on the litter.

After a time he and Bud towed the trailer down to the south turn to load what was left of the Cooper.

Two hours later, Dr. Clark telephoned Cotton at the track. "Is he going to be okay?" Cotton asked.

"I think so. His crash helmet saved his life. It was worn right through where he slid on it after the car turned over. If all goes well, we'll move him to a local hospital tomorrow or the next day. I've called his parents."

"Will you have to stay there?"

"I'll stay with him tonight and drive back tomorrow. Bud's all right, isn't he?" Dr. Clark asked.

"Sure. He's okay."

"What about your car?"

"That's another story," Cotton said.

Mako's crew was checking damage to the Special. The

roll bar had taken most of the impact when the car flipped. The front suspension was ruined and the tail caved in. As Bud and Cotton approached, they saw Al Stubbings arrive in shirt sleeves with his curly blond hair tousled. Mako looked up.

"Did you reach Partmann?" he asked quickly.

Stubbings eloquently raised and dropped his hands. "The sorehead," he growled. "I don't think he could have gotten back to the coast in time to drive next week, anyway. I even put in a call to Earl Fallon. He went over to Gardena Speedway today, his wife said."

Mako looked hopeful. "Is he driving again?"

"No. She let me know he's still in retirement."

At that moment, Stubbings saw the boys standing near the car. As Cotton started on, the promoter moved into their path. He wore a frown of seeming concern as he looked Bud over.

"You okay?" he asked.

Bud nodded. Gil Mako chuckled. "You can't hurt a driver Bud's size. He fits right under the roll bar."

Stubbings asked questions about Red, and Cotton told him what he had learned. Then he said:

"Where's Franks?"

"In the office having a beer," Mako said. "He's kind of shook up."

"He should be. The whole mess was his fault."

Stubbings spoke calmly and reasonably. "The car was leaking a little oil, Cotton, but that wasn't what caused it. I had an Association man look at the surface of the track after the race. He tells me it wasn't the track at all."

"It was slippery enough under Red's tires, where the oil was spraying," Cotton retorted. "He crashed, didn't he?"

"Actually," Mako said thoughtfully, "Red was driving 'way over his head. I've been getting after him about it lately."

"You have?" said Bud.

"He just wasn't ready for all that power.—Charlie says we'll be ready to roll again for Riverside," Mako added. "How's your bucket look?"

Cotton shrugged.

Mako smiled at Bud. "No use driving with a question mark on your car, when you can do it with a dollar sign. Want to drive the Special?"

Bud said quietly. "I wouldn't drive a golden chariot down Main Street, if your name was on it. I've seen you drive with your hook, and I've seen old movies of you winning the Five Hundred. And you look like a carnie tramp any way they run the film. You're a live fossil from the days when they wore linen helmets and drove with a mechanic. And you just put a boy in the hospital encouraging him to drive the old style. No, thanks."

The boys walked on, hearing Mako's friends arguing with him as he tried to follow.

CHAPTER 24 GOOD LUCK SUNDAY

On Thursday, Cotton and Bud went to visit Red at Seaside Hospital, in La Costa. "Ten minutes," a nurse whispered, as she left the room. The head of Red's bed was tilted so that, although he could not sit up, he could look at them. They talked about how good he looked—comparatively—and exaggerated the possibility of his driving again before summer was over.

Red smiled wanly. "Not in the sprints," he said. "Not this child. My folks found out about drivers having to be twenty-one."

It ought to be Mako in this bed, instead of Red, Cotton reflected. "How're you feeling?" he asked.

Red touched the white gauze turban around his head. "I'll give you a rough idea," he said. "A while ago a fly landed on this bandage, and I've still got a headache from him stamping around."

"You'll probably grow up to be an idiot now, being dropped on your head like that," Bud agreed.

Red frowned at the ceiling and then said slowly: "Maybe I was an idiot before it happened . . . ."

"Why?" Cotton said. "Seems to me you've been doing pretty good."

"Maybe I was driving a little over my head," Red said. "I don't know–Mako said to drive as hard as I wanted. I thought I was doing okay. But I should have been able to come out of that spin better than I did."

"*Nobody* could have come out of that spin, Red," Bud told him. "The track was oiled up. The starter should have stopped the race."

Red closed his eyes for a moment. "How's the Cooper?" he asked.

"Mostly body damage. Herb had everything magnafluxed and there aren't any cracks. Looks like we'll run."

"Good. I wonder who's going to drive the Special?"

"Don't know. We thought maybe you'd heard."

"Nobody from the team's been to see me," Red said. "Except Charlie, and I couldn't have visitors that day."

"They're probably working night and day trying to get the car back in shape," Cotton assured him.

Red's hand moved on the blanket. "Wonder if Gil will drive it?"

"I don't see how he could, Red," Bud said. "Fifty laps of hard driving with one hand?"

"Don't sell him short. He's got more muscles in that one arm than most men have in both. He works an hour a day strengthening his muscles. He's got a big ball of silly-putty he squeezes to strengthen his hand, and he lifts dumbbells. He's sure full of the old try."

The nurse came back and looked at them. Cotton and Bud stood up. Red smiled and gave them a salute.

"Good luck Sunday," he said. "Every Sunday. You guys deserve to win."

On Saturday, with Herb driving the old Dodge Power-Wagon and the boys following in Cotton's roadster, they made the hundred-mile trip north to Riverside. Shortly before they reached the huge new raceway, the thunder of sprint cars began to come to them. It raised the short hairs on Cotton's neck like the blare of bugles.

At the track, they used most of their remaining funds to pay their fees. Bud got in some practice laps that afternoon, and Cotton and Herb sought disaster in the many small corners of the car where it liked to hide.

They spent the night in a motel, but were back early Sunday to continue their preparations. By midmorning there was nothing left to do but worry. At last the loud-speaker boomed out their number, and Bud headed down the track.

Cotton and Herb stood on the truck bed to watch him. ". . . Ain't he kind of weaving?" Herb asked, anxiously.

"No, the truck's rocking," Cotton said, with a grin.

Herb was out of practice for race-watching. The car *always* looked as if something was about to go wrong.

"I keep thinking about that front end," Herb confessed. "I know it's foolish, but—"

"Tell you how to keep from thinking about it: think about brakes."

Circling the track at a blistering speed, Bud drove a perfect lap. When he came back, they questioned him about the car's behavior as though he were an astronaut returned from outer space.

"Everything's perfect," he said.

So all they could do was dust the car again, top off the fuel, and check the tire pressure. It was too easy: Cotton suspected disaster was looming over them.

They had forgotten about the Mako team. But now the Special was going out on the track, and they suddenly craned their necks to see who was driving. The announcer said two words, and the stands broke into applause:

"Gil Mako!"

During the time Mako was on the track, there was hardly a sound but the roar of his automobile. He drove a path so perfect an architect might have laid it out. He skidded right up to the wall after each turn, and came off it at the precise instant for maximum speed in the next turn. The blue car finished its lap and coasted into the infield.

"He drives like a saint," Herb sighed. "Can't knock him there."

"Does he always hug the rail like that?" Bud asked. "He looked as though he was glued to it."

"Always. Let anybody try to pass inside, and there's a battle."

Bud rubbed his nose. "But if you tried to pass him outside, he'd probably knock you off the track."

"*Probably*! He majored in Illegal Maneuvers, according to the Association's thumbnail biography of him."

"Maybe I'll have to drive right over him, then," Bud reflected.

"Forget it," Herb said tartly. "Wait for the breaks and drive a sensible race. If we don't win today, we'll win tomorrow."

"What's tomorrow? 'With me, it's always today.' Gil Mako said it." Bud's face crinkled into a grin; but Cotton saw behind it a harsh determination.

"Where did we fail him, Herb?" he said. "Now he's quoting Mako! I'd better wheel the car out myself."

"Relax," Bud said. "I'm saying he needs a shellacking, and this is going to be the day he gets it."

"Okay, but easy does it."

Bud winked at Herb. "Sometimes," he told Cotton, "you sound like two guys. I used practically the same words when you were heading for Phoenix, and you hung up on me."

"That was different," Cotton said. "I've got responsibilities now. I've quit believing in miracles like winning the Western States championship overnight, too. The only miracle I believe in is the way an intelligent mule can outrun a race horse, when the track's heavy."

"So long, mule," Bud said, "I've got to get my rest before the race."

They watched Mako lead four cars out in the trophy dash. He drove with a kind of grim rage, hitting the turns as though they were personal enemies. No one who watched him roar into a corner would ever forget the breathtaking excitement of waiting for his car to break loose and crash into the wall. But it never did. He won the race with plenty of daylight, and walked back to his crew.

Cotton watched him sitting on a rear wheel of his car, smoking thoughtfully with the goggles hanging about his neck as he planned his race. In his black and white coveralls and Wellington boots, he looked leather-tough and confident. For him, the problem was simple: start in front and stay in front. And that was what he had always done best.

A track official came by, breathless and perspiring. "Contestants for the feature race on the track!"

Cotton felt as though he were carrying a bowl of cracked ice in his stomach. He helped Bud with his safety harness, while Herb rounded up a truck to push the car to the track. A few minutes later the field of twelve automobiles was growling about the oval behind Mako's blue pace-setter. Far back in the fourth-row fumes gleamed the orange ember of the car that couldn't happen.

CHAPTER 25 GREAT DAY

After two false starts, the green flag fell. Twelve drivers stomped on their accelerators. Twelve cars leaped out with a single earsplitting detonation. They streaked down the straightaway, cut power, and roared into the turn. Hub to hub, backfiring as they decelerated, they reached the far side of the track and opened up again.

On the chutes, tiny wedges of daylight began to appear. Mako was lengths ahead, the supercharged howl of his engine echoing back across the infield. Billy Michaels, driving his yellow car, was a half-second behind. A contest was going on for third and fourth places, but the Cooper was still walled in by black spinning rubber back in the tangle of slower-running cars.

For four laps there was little change of position. Mako's lead stretched to three seconds, but Michaels had shaken loose and was trying to close the gap. Back in the clods, Bud waited for a favorable situation to develop, a good broken field to weave through like a scatback ball carrier. And while he waited, the front-running cars crept farther and farther ahead.

At lap ten there was a full half-lap between the leaders and the rest of the field.

"What are those clowns doing?" Cotton groaned. "Waiting for the signals to change?"

Then there was a stir of activity. As the pack streamed by, Cotton could see Bud ramming a silver car ahead of him with angry persistence. He kept this up for a full lap; finally things began to loosen. The silver racer stepped up its pace. A white car at Bud's right hung back, leaving a tiny opening. Bud swung outside, drove the next turn high and fast, and came out ahead.

The S-M Special roared past the grandstand on its fifteenth lap, and Gil Mako waved his hook. The crowd applauded, admiring his spirit. There couldn't be too much wrong with a man who had courage like that. He had to be a fine person, a speed chauffeur in the best tradition of the sport. Except that he had sold his integrity for a trophy before he was old enough to shave.

Bud moved up to fifth place, got boxed in, and began jarring at the car on the rail. In a short time the driver increased his speed and a moment later the car skidded from the rail into the loose dirt near the crashwall. The Chopper leaped for the opening. Leaving the turn, its big engine opened up with a high buzz-saw wail.

Bud started after a gold and white car in third position. At the thirty-seventh lap he was close enough to start pressing to pass. At the thirty-ninth he was still trying it high and low and being held off by an expert.

"Time's running out," Herb moaned. "If he hadn't got boxed in, I really think we could've taken 'em."

"It's not over yet," Cotton said.

White smoke suddenly bloomed from the exhaust pipes of the gold car. Backfiring loudly, it began to lose speed. Bud swerved as the car limped toward the infield. With a pagan blare of power, The Chopper now went after the yellow second-place car.

Michaels was holding his position but seemingly not attempting to overtake Mako. As the Cooper closed in, he glanced back and crowded on a little more power. He was working under pressure; the orange car was stealing up on him and there was nothing he could do to stop it. He was traveling at the absolute frontier of safety for his car, and he was too wise to cross it.

Bud caught Michaels in the back turn. He swung high as the yellow car went in tight; Michaels figured the rail was the shortest way around the corner, that Bud's moving outside was a feint.

That was where he was wrong.

Bud stayed at the edge of the loose dirt, then opened up and emerged even with the other car. The grandstand rocked with noise. Michaels crept a few feet ahead, but as the cars streaked down the straightaway The Chopper continued gaining until the drivers were shoulder to shoulder.

Michaels slowed for the turn. Bud pulled ahead, braked hard and took the rail.

Second place.

Mako looked back, and the blue car uttered a rising howl as he responded to the threat. On the next turn he nearly lost his car as his rear wheels pushed his front and he lost traction. With a fine display of car handling, he brought the car under control. But he had lost seconds by the error, and in addition he had proved something that every racing man in the stadium knew beyond doubt.

He was driving the slower car.

Every racing machine had a built-in speed limit. Break it, and nothing but cables could keep you on the track. Mako realized that he had almost crossed that sacred line, that despite his big car and his heavy foot, the little hybrid in back was going to catch him. For over forty laps the slower cars in the pack had kept the Cooper from reaching him. But now the orange car was loose; the contest was between the two of them.

That did not mean the Cooper was going to pass.

Mako held the same searing pace, but made no further attempt to pile up a lead. Bud crept up on him until he was in passing position. With five laps remaining, he suddenly went wide. Mako swung over to block him. Bud attempted to cut back, but the veteran cut him off.

On the forty-seventh lap, Bud bumped the blue car viciously. Mako never budged. Bud tried the inside and the outside, and Mako held him off. On the forty-eighth lap, Bud suddenly started the turn high while Mako went in tight, as usual. The Cooper began to gain on him. Cotton pounded Herb on the back as the orange car moved up. Mako suddenly headed wide to block the Cooper. In the same instant, Bud dropped back a foot or two and dived for the rail.

Mako savagely dropped down on him. Once more Bud had to fall back. Cotton almost wept.

On the forty-ninth lap, Bud seemed to hang back to catch his breath. But as they got the white flag, he came up fast to start nerfing the Special. The turn loomed; Mako went to the rail. Again Bud went high, locking the power on until Cotton feared he could not slow in time to negotiate the turn. At last he braked and put the car into a slide, wheel to wheel with the blue machine and somehow maintaining traction.

Seeing Bud gaining, Mako began to drift into his path. But he was too late to block him without fouling. Cotton uttered an angry yell as the veteran continued moving over, forcing Bud into the wall. Bud grimly stayed with him. Cotton held his breath, certain that Mako could not hold the track at that speed. And if he skidded, he would slam into the Cooper.

Then, subtly, the angle of the blue car changed. Cotton frowned. Had he imagined it? His heart began to thump, as he saw the tail of the blue sprinter swing out just a hair. There was something odd about the angle of the front wheels, too. All in a second, it broke loose.

The car spun sideways, sliding for the wall. As it slid, its front wheel clashed against the Cooper's left rear.

The Special began a mad pinwheel as Mako struggled to master it.

The Chopper headed wildly for the barrier. It struck rear-end first and bounced off, spun around and tried to ram the wall with its front end. Bud crossed the wheels over. The torpedo-nose skimmed along the wall.

A few yards behind, Mako hit the wall solidly. The Special flew apart like a spring-loaded toy. The hood was flying through the air; a wheel rolled across the track. The car went up on its side and began to flip with a terrible clanking. Cotton counted three rolls before it righted itself and crippled across the track.

The little orange car seemed to leave the crashwall reluctantly, as though hating farewells. By some dexterous wheel handling, Bud straightened it out. Billy Michaels roared past Mako's ruined car and rushed up on the Cooper. Bud banged on full power. Michaels' attack was blocked as Bud held him off. The Cooper sprinted ahead, made the back turn smoothly, and went under the checkered flag.

It was dark when they left the track. Clean-up crews were collecting trash by floodlight. The last of the racing cars had been towed away.

"You'd better drive," Bud had said. "I'm still blind from flashbulbs."

Photographers from all the speed magazines had taken shots of the Cooper, its pilot, and mechanics. Even the haughty sports car journals snapped a few pictures and asked some questions. Herb borrowed Cotton's roadster and left early, full of a kind of energy Cotton had seldom observed in him.

"Excuse me, kids—got a lot of wrecking yards to hit in L.A. tomorrow. There's going to be a run on European cars that'll make the gold rush look like a sack race. You're looking at the future demolished-sports-car king of the West. I'm putting in buy-orders at every yard in the county."

South of town, the highway ran straight and smooth through rocky hills, white-ribbed in the moonlight. Far ahead ruby taillights gleamed on a hill, where cars wound up a grade.

"How about that Mako character?" Cotton said. "Losing the same hand twice. Lucky for him it was made of steel this time."

When Bud was silent, Cotton glanced at him. Wedged into a corner of the cab, he had fallen asleep. Cotton smiled. Bud had burned up a lot of energy today. So had Mako, but the Old Pro wouldn't sleep tonight. He had taken a severe bruising out there, and something vital in him had been left for dead. His pride—the pride of a man who had worn his ego like a medal and had it ripped away. Tonight Mako was just a has-been with a fund of moth-eaten war stories.

What had he tried to buy with his twenty years of racing? Cotton wondered. Glory? Whatever he had wanted, his total contribution to the world of speed consisted of a line of flags fluttering in the breeze like checkered laundry. Yesterday's win flags.

Yet perhaps a somewhat tarnished reputation was enough for an old warhorse like Mako. Not for me,

Cotton realized. Nor for the racing people who never drove a lap, but dreamed of capturing the wind and pressing it into the shape of a racing car. For men like that, the glory trail started at a drawing board and ended in a garage.

He dreamed.

Indianapolis Speedway. Daytona. Springfield. "*—The first three cars finishing were powered by the new Clark engine. . . .*" "*—Cotton Clark's revolutionary fuel injector helped A. J. Foyt set a new track record of . . . .*"

Then he frowned, with a premonition of trigonometry and slide rules. Still, there was a price tag on everything. Perhaps it was no worse to stay in school a few years longer than to view the world from a wrecking yard, knowing that with a little more education you could have been designing engines for race cars. For if he had learned nothing else this year, he had learned that shortcuts and miracles happened mostly when you were asleep.

ABOUT THE AUTHOR

As he gathered background material for *Speedway Contender,* Frank Bonham watched auto races and spoke with many drivers and mechanics. He crewed for the driver of a three-quarter midget racer, although his duties were limited to pouring fuel and pushing the car to get it started. One thing which continually impressed him was the seriousness of all the people involved. He writes, "The mechanics are skilled men making good money at their trade of rebuilding and repairing cars in hours. . . . Sometimes an engine will be torn down and rebuilt overnight to correct some fault the driver has noticed in practice." Mr. Bonham decided that someone should say a good word for the youngsters who work harder at their hobby than most of their parents ever worked at one, and this became the theme of his story.

Frank Bonham has written several short stories and novels—for both adults and children. He lives in La Jolla, California, with his wife and three sons.